Jackie Ashenden writes dark, emotional stories, with alpha heroes who've just got the world to their liking only to have it blown wide apart by their kick-ass heroines. She lives in Auckland, New Zealand, with her husband, the inimitable Dr Jax, two kids and two rats. When she's not torturing alpha males and their gutsy heroines she can be found drinking chocolate martinis, reading anything she can lay her hands on, wasting time on social media or being forced to go mountain biking with her husband. To keep up to date with Jackie's new releases and other news sign up to her newsletter at jackieashenden.com.

Also by Jackie Ashenden

Crowned at the Desert King's Command
The Spaniard's Wedding Revenge
The Italian's Final Redemption
The World's Most Notorious Greek
The Innocent Carrying His Legacy

**The Royal House of Axios
miniseries**

Promoted to His Princess
The Most Powerful of Kings

Discover more at millsandboon.co.uk.

THE
WEDDING NIGHT
THEY NEVER HAD

JACKIE ASHENDEN

MILLS & BOON

First published in Great Britain 2021
by Mills & Boon, an imprint of HarperCollins*Publishers* Ltd,
1 London Bridge Street, London, SE1 9GF

www.harpercollins.co.uk

HarperCollins*Publishers*
1st Floor, Watermarque Building,
Ringsend Road, Dublin 4, Ireland

Large Print edition 2021

The Wedding Night They Never Had © 2021 Jackie Ashenden

ISBN: 978-0-263-28917-6

12/21

MIX
Paper from
responsible sources
FSC **FSC** C007454

This book is produced from independently certified
FSC™ paper to ensure responsible forest management.
For more information visit www.harpercollins.co.uk/green.

Printed and bound in the UK using 100% Renewable
Electricity at CPI Group (UK) Ltd, Croydon, CR0 4YY

When the wind stops and, over the heavens,
The clouds go, nevertheless,
In their direction.
—*The Death of a Soldier* by Wallace Stevens

PROLOGUE

PRINCE CASSIUS DE LEON, second in line to the throne of Aveiras, sat in his limo after a hard night's partying and contemplated his choices. Outside, four women waited, all beautiful and all eager to be his companion for the night.

He wasn't going to rush choosing one, however. He liked to take his time when it came to deciding on his bed partners, because there were many important things to take into account.

Would the delicious brunette with the hot, dark eyes turn out to be passionate or shy? Would the curvy redhead with the infectious smile let him lead the way? Perhaps the tall, Amazonian blonde would be more demanding than the other brunette, the one with the dirty laugh, but did he feel like 'demanding'? Or did he want someone more low-key?

It was a difficult decision; he didn't like to disappoint and someone was going to have to miss out. Though…maybe not. He could have all four. He was, after all, feeling quite energetic tonight.

At that moment, the door to the limo opened and a fairy got in.

Cassius blinked.

No, not a fairy, but a tiny, fragile-looking woman wearing the shortest, most clinging black mini-dress in the history of creation. She was very pale, with long, silvery white hair that hung to her waist, and she stared at him from under lids heavy with garish blue eyeshadow and lashes gone spidery with inexpertly applied mascara. Her eyes were a luminous grey and the biggest he'd ever seen.

He blinked again.

No, not a woman. A girl. A teenage girl.

Cassius frowned. What the hell was a teen-age girl doing climbing into his limo? It wasn't entirely unheard of, but his staff was usually better at weeding out people who shouldn't be approaching him.

'Your Highness,' the girl said earnestly. 'I'm sorry. I know this is quite rude, but…um… well… I really need you to ruin me.'

Cassius blinked a third time. 'What?'

'I need you to ruin me. Quite urgently, in fact.

Tonight.' She glanced nervously out the window. 'Right now, if possible.'

It was true that his reputation as a notorious womaniser was well-earned and he was famous for never saying no to anything that might prove to be enjoyable. However, that did not extend to teenage girls. And, if this one thought he customarily ruined teenagers, then his reputation was even worse than he'd thought.

Won't your father be proud?

Cassius did not appreciate this thought so he ignored it.

'First things first,' he said, giving her a narrow stare. 'How old are you?'

'Twenty.' Her grey eyes shone. 'I'm not a child.'

He sighed. 'Of course you're a child. And, sadly for you, I'm not a pervert. Get out of the limo, little one. I have actual women to see tonight.'

The sprite frowned then reached into the tiny silver mesh bag slung over one narrow shoulder, pulled out a pair of glasses, rubbed the lenses on her dress then put them on her pert nose.

'Look,' she said very seriously, 'You don't have to do anything to me. I only need everyone else to think that you have.'

Cassius knew he should open the limo door and get one of his guards to get rid of her, and he couldn't think why he wasn't doing so now, especially when he had several delicious beauties all ready and waiting for the crook of his finger. But he was curious about, not to mention intrigued by, her boldness. It took guts to climb into the limo of a prince of Aveiras, automatically assuming he wouldn't simply throw her out.

He stretched out his legs and shoved his hands in his pockets. 'I assume you're going to tell me why you need everyone to think I've taken a sudden liking to teenagers?'

Her forehead creased. 'I'm not a teenager. Anyway, the reason is that my parents want me to marry this horrible, abusive man. But, if word gets out that I've spent the night with Prince Cassius, he'll know I'm not a virgin any more and he won't want me.'

Cassius waited for her to offer more, but she didn't. So he opened his mouth to issue a gentle but firm refusal when she added, 'The man is Stefano Castelli.'

Cassius closed his mouth.

Stefano Castelli was the head of one of the

old aristocratic families. He was fifty if he was a day, childless since his wife had died some years before, and he'd made no secret of the fact that he was in the market for a new wife to deliver him heirs. What he did keep secret was the rumours of his...unorthodox sexual tastes. The man was a monster and, if this child was given to him in marriage, she wouldn't stay a child much longer.

'What's your name?' he asked, curious, because if an arranged marriage was on the cards she must come from one of Aveiras's aristocratic families.

'Inara Donati.' She gave him an owlish look. 'Well? Will you help me?'

He hadn't heard of the Donatis. Then again, he'd never paid attention to the interminable lessons about royal protocol his father had put him and his brother through when they'd been children which, among other things, had required memorising the list of important Aveiran families.

Perhaps the Donatis were part of the nouveau riche who were desperate to claim links to the aristocracy in order to bolster their own social standing. Aveirans were notoriously snobbish when it came to their lineages and arranged marriages were common. Though they didn't usually start them off that young.

Whatever the case, if what she said was true—and she probably wasn't lying—then marrying off this child to Stefano Castelli was nothing short of criminal.

Cassius seldom stirred himself for others, because he was nothing if not committed to his life of supreme self-indulgence, but he didn't like that thought. At all.

'I need more information,' he said. 'Your real age, for example.'

She looked irritated by this. 'I don't see how—'

'If you please,' Cassius commanded.

The girl pulled a face. 'Okay, fine. I'm sixteen.'

It wasn't illegal to be married at sixteen, not if you had your parents' permission, or in this case your parents' insistence.

'I see,' he said carefully. 'And why are they so set on the marriage?'

'Because the Castellis are an old family and my parents want to be part of the aristocracy.' Inara fiddled with her bag. 'Is that all?'

'What about other family members who could

help you? Or friends, perhaps?' It was a perfectly reasonable question, but he thought he knew the answer to that already.

She shook her head. 'I'm an only child and no one will stand up to my father.'

A difficult situation. Even more difficult when her parents had a legal responsibility for her until she turned eighteen.

You could help her, though. No one will say no to a prince. And perhaps this is your chance to show your father what you're made of.

Cassius didn't care what his father thought of him, but the old man had been on his back about his behaviour recently and it was getting tiresome. Because, while it was true that when his brother ascended the throne Cassius would be expected to be his right-hand man, Cassius wasn't going to be king himself, so why should he have to conform?

Still, this girl had come to him for help, and she was looking at him as if he was her saviour. This was something of a novelty, when his family tended to view him as the disappointment he was, while his lovers were only hungry for the pleasure he could bring them.

No one looked at him as though he could save

them, as though he was the answer to all their prayers.

He liked it.

Except…being this girl's saviour would be difficult. She was under age, and therefore still under her parents' guardianship, and, though he might be able to find her a refuge, if her parents claimed her he wouldn't be able to stop them. No one was above the law, not even royalty.

There was the police, but the filing of reports took time, as did investigations into abuse allegations, and that was probably time this girl didn't have.

He could ask the King for help, of course, but his father never looked kindly on his activities. Besides, a small piece of him didn't want to ask his father for help anyway. A small piece of him wanted to save this girl himself.

Yet how? If he could somehow become her legal guardian, that would be ideal, but also impossible, considering her parents were still alive.

The girl frowned at him. 'It's easy. All you have to do is keep me for a couple of hours and everyone will think—'

'Everyone will think that my tastes run to under-age girls and, while it's true that I don't care much about my reputation, I care enough not to want rumours like that attached to my name.'

She bit her lip. 'Oh. I hadn't thought of that.'

'Clearly.' He kept his tone dry. 'Also, I'm afraid that, while virginity might be valued in some circles, I'm pretty sure Stefano Castelli wouldn't care if you were one or not. He just wants heirs.'

Her forehead creased, a line appearing in the smooth skin between her brows. She looked... anxious. No, more than that. She looked scared.

'Then what should I do?' Desperation suddenly glowed in her eyes. 'I could leave the country. I could—'

'Where would you go?' he interrupted gently. 'You have no passport, I'm assuming, and no money. And, even if you did, the courts would soon make sure you were sent back to your family.'

She took a soft breath and looked away, blinking hard. It was obvious she was trying hard not to cry. 'Then,' she said in a shaky voice, 'I suppose I have no choice. I'm sorry, Your Highness. I'd better go.'

But Cassius had already made a decision. She was distressed and in danger, and she'd come to him for help. Not to his brother, the noble heir who could do no wrong, but to *him*.

To her he wasn't the dissolute, no-good second son. To her he wasn't a careless, self-centred playboy prince.

To her he was a hero…her potential saviour.

So that was who he'd be.

'Wait,' he said, his brain moving at lightning speed, sorting through all the most likely options and then discarding them.

There was only one way he could think of to become her guardian. Only way to save her from marriage to a monster and to keep her parents happy at the same time.

He'd marry her himself.

It was a shocking decision that would likely appal his parents, and there'd no doubt be a scandal. But that was too bad. He'd never be the kind of prince they wanted him to be and he'd long since given up trying.

He'd be a hero for this girl instead.

And as for her parents, well, they'd probably be delighted to have a prince for a son-in-law instead of some minor lord.

He'd offer her the protection of his name and,

in essence, she'd be his ward. He'd look after her until she reached her legal majority.

Two years. That was all it would be. And then they'd divorce and she'd be out of her parents' clutches for ever.

It was unorthodox, certainly, but the main thing was that she'd be safe. And *he* would be the one to save her.

She was looking at him with big eyes, as if her entire existence waited on his next word.

Which it did.

'There is one way I can help you.' He met her gaze very directly. 'But I'm afraid you might not like it.'

'It can't be any worse than having to marry Stefano Castelli,'

'That depends,' Cassius said. 'How do you feel about marrying me instead?'

CHAPTER ONE

'HIS MAJESTY HAS arrived, Your Majesty.'

Inara looked up from the email she'd been in the middle of excitedly typing to a colleague in Helsinki and blinked at Henri, her elderly butler. 'What? Already?'

Used to her absent-minded lapses when it came to time, the butler inclined his head. 'Indeed, Your Majesty. He's in the lavender sitting room.'

Inara's heartbeat accelerated. The lavender sitting room wasn't the tidiest room in the Queen's Estate and she knew her husband valued order. Henri and his wife Joan kept the estate in reasonable order, but it wouldn't be up to the King's standards.

How awful.

Inara felt her face get hot. She shoved back her chair and stood up quickly, her heart beating even faster. Even now her palms felt sweaty and her breath was short.

It was always this way whenever he visited. Five years she'd been married, and she was still as in love with him as she'd ever been, while he still barely acknowledged her existence.

No, that was a lie. He used to visit her regularly, shielding her from the scandal that their marriage had caused, then making sure she'd been looked after as the years had gone by. 'The Prince's Forgotten Wife', the press had dubbed her, which was fine. She didn't care.

He'd protected her from her parents with his name and his power, allowing her to finish school and attend university, pursuing her interest in mathematics. Most of the time he left her alone, though he'd used to visit for dinner or sometimes lunch, a breakfast here and there, and they'd talk, discussing all manner of subjects.

She'd loved those visits. She'd had him all to herself.

Then, two years after their marriage, his entire family had been killed in an accident and he'd become King. And the visits had stopped.

Inara wiped her hands on her dress unthinkingly. 'Oh dear, I know I left about a thousand teacups in there, and I—'

'It's all tidy,' Henri interrupted in that fatherly way he had. 'Don't fret, Your Majesty.'

Inara gave him a grateful smile then half-raised her hand to her hair, wondering vaguely if she should do anything about it, before lowering it as Henri gave a small shake of his head.

No time to change or fuss with her appearance. The King didn't like to be kept waiting.

Inara moved around the side of her desk and into the wide hallway that ran the length of the little manor house. She'd moved here from Katara, the capital, when Cassius had ascended the throne. The traditional holiday estate of the queens of Aveiras, it was buried deep in the countryside amongst farmland and ancient forests, and she loved it for its isolation and privacy. Here, she was away from the city and its frenetic pace that disturbed her thinking, and away from the glare of the press and the eyes of the world that always made her feel small and plain and inadequate.

Cassius had only visited her a couple of times since he'd been crowned, preferring her to come to the city whenever there were royal duties to carry out as his queen. It made her wonder why he was here now.

Her stomach twisted in a sudden attack of nerves, but she swallowed it down. She didn't want anything to ruin her joy at seeing him.

The door to the sitting room was open, so she went right in. Her husband stood before the fireplace with his back to her, a tall, broad statue in a dark suit. His hands were clasped behind his back, the royal seal of Aveiras gleaming on the middle finger of his right hand, his plain gold wedding band gleaming on the ring finger of his left.

Even with his back to her, he dominated the room.

Inara's chest tightened, her stomach doing its usual swoop and dive, like the starlings over the south field in the evenings.

It was always the same whenever she was in his vicinity. She got hot and jittery, and her brain wouldn't work. She also couldn't stop staring at him.

She tried to hide her reaction to him, because she wasn't sixteen any more, but she suspected he knew anyway. He was an experienced, much older man and, regrettably, not stupid. However, he never mentioned it, for which she was grateful, pretending not to notice her stutters and her sweaty palms, and coolly tolerant of her lapses into vagueness.

Really, it was a blessing she only saw him occasionally.

Inara pushed her glasses up her nose, took a breath and opened her mouth to welcome him.

'How are you, Inara?' he asked before she could get words out. He kept his back to her, his gaze on the watercolour of a vivid lavender field that hung above the fireplace and gave the room its name.

His voice was deep and cool, flowing over her heated skin like river water on a hot summer's day.

'Oh…um…good.' Distractedly, she rubbed her hands down the sides of her cotton dress. 'I've been chatting with Professor Koskinen in Helsinki about a theory I've been working on. It's really interesting. I've had look at some of the—'

'I'm sure you have.' He continued to examine the painting in front of him. 'But I'm afraid I'm not here to discuss your theories.'

Stop babbling and start acting like a normal person.

Inara closed her mouth hard against the urge

to chatter, her joy at seeing him fading somewhat. 'Why are you here, then?

Slowly he turned around to face her and Inara's heart clenched like a fist.

Cassius de Leon, King of Aveiras, was quite simply the most beautiful man she'd ever met, and she lost the power of speech whenever he was near. At six-four, he towered above most men, and was built broad and muscular, like a mediaeval warrior. His hair was coal-black and his eyes were dark amber, his features possessing a fierce, compelling masculine beauty that captivated everyone he met.

When she'd first met him, he'd been a notorious playboy with a wicked streak a mile wide, and a charming smile that had granted him access to bedrooms and hearts all over Europe and beyond.

Those days were over, however. Now, that charm rarely made an appearance, and wickedness not at all. There was only a steady, cool authority that made most of his court, not to mention parliament, cower before him.

The notorious playboy prince was gone, leaving in his place a rigid and unbending king.

The King who was her husband.

Inara gritted her teeth against the urge to kneel before him that always gripped her whenever she was confronted with him. She'd done so once, the day of his coronation, and he'd told her to get up. Queens didn't kneel, so she'd tried not to give in to the urge.

That didn't stop it happening, however.

With difficulty, she met his gaze.

'It's quite simple,' the King said. 'I'm here because I want a divorce.'

Cassius was expecting his wife to nod in her usual absent-minded way and tell him that a divorce was fine, before offering him a cup of tea and launching into a conversation about whatever thing was holding her interest at that moment. Six months ago, when he'd last visited, she'd been talking about dark matter and he'd been lost within minutes.

To be fair, that might have had more to do with how she'd been wearing a ridiculously filmy white shirt through which he'd been able to see her lacy bra, and he'd been far too distracted for his own good.

Another reason—as if he needed yet another—why a divorce was a good idea.

Except this time Inara didn't nod in her usual absent-minded way. Her pretty elfin features went pale and her small, perfect rosebud of a mouth opened in what looked like shock.

'A…divorce?' Her voice, usually sweet and clear, now sounded husky.

She looked as if he'd stabbed her and he wasn't quite sure what to make of that. They'd agreed they'd divorce when she legally became an adult at eighteen, but then his brother and his parents had died, he'd become King and everything had gone to hell in a handcart.

A divorce had been the last thing he'd wanted to think about and it had been the last thing the country had needed after the shock death of its king and heir. Stability and normality was what Aveiras had needed so that was what he'd delivered.

But three years had passed since then and, now the country had recovered, it was time to shore it up by producing an heir. His ministers were very insistent about it and he couldn't argue with them. Cassius was the only surviving member of his family so securing his legacy with children—and lots of them—was imperative.

He needed a woman who could be a real wife

to him, who could provide him with the heirs he required and who could take her place at his side as a proper queen. Someone who could meet heads of state and hold her own at royal functions, who had the authority, grace, and dignity of Aveiras's previous queen, his mother. And, most importantly, someone who was not the teenage girl he'd married when he'd been young and stupid, still thinking that he could be somebody's saviour. That saving her would prove that he wasn't as selfish as his father had always believed him to be.

Inara's misty grey eyes were huge behind the lenses of her glasses, her fingers curled into fists. She wore a loose, white cotton dress that was as filmy as the shirt she'd worn the last time, and the material was transparent enough for him to see her underwear. Her knickers were lacy and dark-blue, her bra lacy and purple.

He shouldn't be looking. His days of being led around by his baser appetites were over and done with. They'd died along with his brother.

Inara's hair was in its usual messy tumble of silvery white curls that hung to her waist and it looked as though she hadn't brushed it. Some of it was tied back from her face with a rubber band. She had a small blue line across one pale cheek, as if she'd accidentally drawn on herself with a pen.

Definitely not queen material.

No, she never had been. And when he'd married her that had been the last thing on his mind.

'But I…' Inara began, still sounding husky. 'Um, I mean, c-can I ask why?'

Of course there would be questions. He'd expected that.

He stared at her impassively. 'To be blunt, I need heirs. And I'm sure you can understand why. Also, Aveiras needs a queen who takes an active interest in the country and who supports me in my duties as King.'

'Oh,' Inara said faintly. 'I…s-see.'

She was still very pale, which was odd. The plan had never been to stay married, and besides, he knew that she didn't like living in the city. That she didn't like being Queen, full-stop. So surely she should be pleased at this news?

'You can keep the Queen's Estate, if that's what you're worried about.' He glanced around the room, noting that, while it had certainly been dusted well, there was still a lot of cheerful clutter everywhere.

The Queen's Estate was a pretty place, but it reminded him too much of his mother, so if Inara wanted it she could have it.

'Or you could take your pick of any royal property, if you prefer,' he went on when she didn't say anything. 'You'll also be given a monthly stipend that should keep you quite comfortable.'

Still she said nothing, continuing to look at him as if he'd hurt her.

'Your life won't change,' he said gently, because her colour hadn't returned and it concerned him. 'You can stay here and continue with your research. You don't have to move if you don't want to. And you won't have to come into Katara any longer.' He paused. 'You'll be free, little one. The way you always wanted to be.'

Yet the shocked expression on her face lingered, and after a moment she looked away, clenching and unclenching her hands.

She definitely was *not* pleased by the news, and he still couldn't understand it. When he'd offered her the protection of his name that night in the limo five years earlier, she'd been wary, and rightly so. She'd wanted to escape a marriage, not jump head-first into another one.

His parents had been horrified, as had the majority of the country after news of the marriage had come out. They hadn't seen him as the saviour he'd hoped they would, and it didn't matter that he'd done it to protect someone else. It had been a scandal attached to the family name and how could he be so selfish? What was one girl compared to the dignity of the crown?

They were right, of course; he hadn't married Inara to save her. He'd married Inara to save himself in his family's eyes. Still, what was done was done, and he'd stubbornly stuck to the story he'd told himself: he'd saved an innocent teenage girl from the clutches of a monster.

However, the necessity of the marriage hadn't existed for three years. He should have started divorce proceedings earlier, but assuming the duties of a position he'd never wanted, and had never envisaged taking on, had consumed most of his time.

'If you're worried about what will happen to you,' he said into the growing silence, 'Then you needn't—'

'I'm not worried about what will happen to me.'

Cassius stared at her.

She kept her attention out of the window, her hands still clenched, her knuckles white. She'd never interrupted him before.

He frowned. 'What's wrong, Inara?'

Agitation poured off her. She'd always been bright and sparky and interested, with a magpie mind that darted here and there. He found her intellectual, yet quirky and amusing, and he enjoyed his visits to check on her progress.

She hadn't seemed to care that he was a prince or a king. She'd been interested in his opinions, not because he was a royal, but because she seemed genuinely interested in him. And she didn't always agree with his views; she was quite happy to argue a point, which he found stimulating, as hardly anyone argued with him any more.

She looked at him all of a sudden, her pointed chin firming as if she'd reached a decision about something.

'No,' she said flatly.

Cassius wasn't sure what she was talking about. 'No? No what?'

Inara's chin came up. 'No, I'm not giving you a divorce.'

CHAPTER TWO

INARA HAD NEVER said no to him, not once. In all the years she'd been married to him, she'd done everything he'd asked. Refusing him wasn't something she'd ever contemplated. He'd saved her from the marriage her parents had tried to force her into and, even though some of the things he'd asked her to do after he'd become King had been annoying and anxiety-producing, she'd done them without hesitation or complaint.

She owed him and, though he might not have said that explicitly, she was fully aware of her debt and was happy to pay it.

So she wasn't sure why she said no now.

She'd always known their marriage wasn't going to be for ever, that eventually he'd gently but firmly disentangle her from his life. She'd expected it at eighteen, but then the royal family had all died in a helicopter crash, leaving Cassius to ascend the throne, and all the divorce plans had fallen by the wayside.

For the past five years she'd been his wife in name only, and she'd been happy. She'd lost herself in the research her parents had never allowed her to undertake, as they didn't view it as helpful to their social-climbing interests, content with burying herself in the glory of numbers and intellectual discussions via email with other researchers and experts.

Sometimes Cassius visited her, and she lived for those visits, yet dreaded them at the same time.

Lived, because she got to see him.

Dreaded, because he treated her the way he had always treated her: as if she was still that sixteen-year-old girl who'd crept into his limo one night.

Even so, she was happy. And a divorce wouldn't change things, as theirs wasn't a proper marriage in the first place. How could it be, when she'd been a child bride and he a notorious playboy prince?

He didn't love her. He didn't want her. He'd married her to rescue her and, now that she was safe, there was no reason for their marriage to continue. None at all.

Yet everything in her rebelled at the thought.

Cassius stood like a statue, a dark, still point in the bright, pretty room. The walls had been painted a parchment colour, and there were watercolours on the walls, all of them echoing that lavender shade, as did the soft velvet of the couch. The furniture, which she'd ordered herself, was as delicate and pretty as the art on the walls, but suddenly all of it seemed flimsy and insubstantial next to him.

His expression hadn't changed, yet Inara was sure that the late-summer sunlight flooding into the room had dimmed and the temperature had dropped.

'Excuse me?' His deep voice was mild. 'Did you just say no, you're not going to give me a divorce?'

He was always composed. Always controlled and cool. He never got angry, never lost his temper. But he never smiled either. He used to smile a lot...

Inara took a slow, steady breath. She should nod her head and give in, tell him that of course he could have a divorce. That he could go and find some other woman who could do all the things he'd said. Who could give him children, support him as a wife should and be the kind of queen Aveiras deserved instead of the absent-minded, overly intellectual, socially inept mess that she was.

She'd always known she didn't have what it took to be a queen, just as she'd always known he'd never feel for her what she felt for him. So, really, she should step aside and let him find someone else to make him happy. Or at least happier than he was.

But you don't want him to find another woman.

That was the problem. She didn't.

'Th-that's right,' she said, annoyed with herself for stuttering. 'I mean, you have a wife already, Your Majesty.'

Cassius's expression remained inscrutable. 'A wife who calls me "Your Majesty" is not the kind of wife I need.'

She blushed. How ridiculous to have called him that. Before he'd become King, she'd called him Cassius, and had had no problem with it. It was only after his family had died that he'd become so reserved and distant, and calling him Cassius had felt too…presumptuous.

'Fine.' She gave him a steady look. 'You already have a wife, *Cassius.*'

'But you're not really my wife, Inara.' His voice,

again, was gentle. 'That was something forced on you, so why wouldn't you want to be rid of me as soon as you can?'

She could tell him the truth—that she was in love with him. That she'd loved him for years and, now that the reality of losing him for ever was staring her in the face, she couldn't stand it.

But what would he say? What would a man like him, a king, want with the love of the girl he'd once rescued and married out of pity?

How can you lose him when you never had him in the first place?

She unclenched her fingers, stretching them to relieve some of her agitation. 'I've enjoyed it, though.'

'Again, what part of your life is connected to mine? Apart from legally?'

She tried to think. 'You…come and visit me.'

'Occasionally, yes. But occasional visits are not enough, and I think you know that.'

Of course she knew that.

'Well…why can't I h-help you out with all those things?'

He frowned. 'Why would you want to do that?' He said it as if it was the most mystifying thing he'd ever heard in his life.

Inara found it irritating. He'd never been quite this patronising before. 'It just seems a little… I don't know…pointless to go looking for some-one when I could, you know, do what ever you need.'

'But I didn't marry you for that,' Cassius said patiently. 'I married you because you needed protection, nothing more.'

'Yes, I know that, but—'

'I will be needing heirs, little one. You do know how children are conceived, don't you?'

The use of his old pet name for her was both irritating and comforting at the same time.

'Yes, of course,' she said testily. 'Believe it or not, Cassius, I'm not sixteen any more. And even when I was sixteen I knew how children were conceived.'

The calm expression on his face didn't change. 'Then you'll understand why it's impossible for you to continue being my wife.'

A needle of hurt pierced her; she was so stu-pid to think he might want her. She'd left herself open for that, hadn't she? Not that she'd truly thought he would, but a part of her had nursed a faint hope.

'I didn't think I was that unattractive,' she said

before she could stop herself. 'But I suppose if it's impossible then I must be.'

'Of course you're not unattractive,' Cassius said. 'But it's not about your attractiveness or otherwise. It's about the fact that I still see you as a sixteen-year-old girl.'

It didn't come as any surprise. He'd always thought of her that way and she knew it.

You haven't done much to change his mind, though, have you?

No, and she hadn't because she…well…she just hadn't. She'd pushed it out of her mind, not wanting to think about when the day would come that he'd need heirs, a proper queen, a life…

A divorce.

But that day was now here and she couldn't ignore it any longer.

You need to do something.

Yes, but what?

'I'm not a sixteen-year-old girl, as I've already pointed out.' She tried to sound as cool as he did. 'I'm twenty-one.'

'Be that as it may, you are still not a suitable prospect for queen.'

Inara took a couple of steps towards him, annoyed now. 'That hasn't been a problem for the last three years. What's changed?'

His amber gaze flicked down her figure and then up again, lightning fast, but there was no alteration in his expression. 'I've been advised it's past time for me to start a family. Aveiras needs heirs, and the sooner the better.'

She understood. The country had lost nearly its entire royal family in one fell swoop, so naturally parliament would want to safeguard the royal line. They'd also want a queen who lived at the palace and took part in royal life, not someone who preferred an isolated country manor and spent most of her time studying arcane mathematical problems.

No, everything about this made logical sense and, given that the pathways of her own mind tended towards the logical, there was no earthly reason why she should refuse to give him the divorce he wanted.

Except that the part of herself she'd never understood and had never wanted to think about too deeply, the part that had fallen desperately in love with her husband, didn't want to.

Her heart wanted to be his queen. It wanted to give him heirs. It wanted to be by his side and support him. It wanted do all the things he'd just said and more, and it was furious he'd even consider choosing someone else.

But what could she say? How could she argue? He still saw her as a child and, as long as he did, nothing would change his mind.

The fizzing happiness of his presence began to recede, a flat feeling stealing through her.

He'd never been a man who changed his mind once he'd made a decision, not even when he'd been that laughing, charming prince, and she knew there was no point arguing with him.

'Fine. I suppose it doesn't matter what I say.' She clasped her trembling hands in front of her. 'You've obviously made your choice. I don't know why you bothered coming here at all, in that case. You could have just sent me an email.'

Another frown flickered over his perfect features. 'An email? You really think I'd ask you for a divorce via email?'

'You haven't visited me in nearly six months. And you've already made up your mind. You could have just sent me an order; you didn't need to make the trek all the way out here.'

Cassius's gaze sharpened. 'You're upset. Why?'

Shock pulsed down her spine. She'd forgotten

how perceptive he could be—when he deigned to notice, that was.

But she couldn't tell him the truth. He'd look at her with distant, condescending pity and tell her gently once again that any kind of relationship between them was impossible. The thought was unbearable.

'I'm not hurt,' she said, forcing away her anger and the small, sharp pain of rejection. 'I'm only…shocked, I suppose. It's quite sudden.'

He gazed at her, still frowning, and she thought he might push it, but as he opened his mouth to speak someone said, 'Your Majesty, we have an issue.'

Inara turned to see one of the uniformed palace aides standing in the doorway to the sitting room.

Cassius straightened. 'What is it, Carlo?'

'There's a mechanical problem with the helicopter. A part needs to be replaced, and we can get it, but it won't be here until after dark.'

If this annoyed him, Cassius didn't show it. His expression remained opaque. 'How long will it take to fix?'

'A couple of hours.' Carlo looked apologetic. 'I'm terribly sorry, Your Majesty, but—'

'It's no problem,' Cassius interrupted. 'I'm sure the Queen won't mind if we stay here the night.'

Inara blinked. 'You want to...what?'

'Flying at night can be an issue and safety is of prime concern to me.' He nodded at Carlo. 'Tell the pilot not to rush. We'll leave first thing tomorrow morning.'

Wait. What was he suggesting?

'T-Tomorrow?'

He glanced at her. 'We'll stay here, obviously. There should be room for everyone.'

Already unsettled, his casual arrogance was a further irritation to her. Sure, he was the King, and casual arrogance was part of the job. And, yes, technically, although it was known as the Queen's Estate, the manor was owned by the crown, thus him. But, still, she'd been living here for three years and she'd come to think of it as hers. He couldn't just arrive, demand a divorce then decide to stay the night, as if having the house full of his presence for the next twelve hours wouldn't be an issue.

Except...how could she argue? He was the King and this, despite all her protests, *was* his house.

Yes, and you're the Queen. Don't forget that.

That was true. She was. Maybe not for too much longer, but she was still the Queen now.

Inara raised her chin and stared at him in what she hoped was a haughty fashion. 'Actually, I'm not sure. I'll have to check.'

Another flicker of expression crossed his perfect features, but whether irritation or impatience she couldn't tell. 'No need. Henri is still managing the house, I imagine? I'll inform him. It's only me, Carlo, the pilot and a couple of my guards.'

Already he was looking away from her. Already he was dismissing her as if her feelings and her opinions were of no consequence.

As if *she* were of no consequence.

It reminded her too much of her parents and the way they'd controlled every aspect of her existence when she'd been young. She hadn't been a daughter to them, only currency. A way to buy themselves more social standing, not a person with hopes and dreams of her own.

Hurt buried itself inside her, making her ache. If she'd needed any more proof that he didn't care about her, then this was it, wasn't it?

What do you expect? He asked you if you were upset and you told him you weren't.

It was true, and she had no one to blame for that but herself.

Inara opened her mouth to tell him that she would have appreciated being asked first, but he'd already moved past her and was issuing further orders to Carlo, leaving her standing there, gaping silently after him.

Cassius entered the small library and stopped, surveying it with some disapproval. The room bore the signs of recent cleaning, yet there were still stacks of papers and books scattered over various surfaces. The sideboard had on it some dead flowers in a vase and what appeared to be several tea cups with different levels of tea in them.

A woollen garment of some kind—a cardigan?—had been thrown carelessly onto one of the leather arm chairs that stood beside the fireplace, and now half of it was trailing on the floor. A single slipper had been kicked under the chair. A few pens sat on the mantelpiece above the fire, along with yet more tea cups.

A disgrace. Was his wife the culprit or did the

fault lie with the staff for not cleaning properly? Not that he could blame the staff, given Henri and Joan were getting on in years. However, had Inara always been this untidy or had he never noticed? It had been six months since he'd last been here, after all.

A thread of something that he refused to call shame coiled through him. It was ridiculous to be ashamed that he hadn't visited her. She might legally be his wife, but there was nothing between them beyond that. He visited her out of a sense of duty, that was all, and, although she was always pleased to see him, she'd never said that she wished she saw more of him. In fact, the few times her presence had been required for any kind of state function in Katara, she'd appeared uncomfortable, awkward and downright miserable, which had led him to believe she only liked to see him when he was scheduled to visit.

Certainly her obvious displeasure with him today had confirmed that theory. True, initiating divorce proceedings wasn't a happy subject, but he hadn't thought she'd be quite so upset. And he definitely hadn't thought she'd care about him staying.

Apparently, he'd been wrong about both of those things.

Cassius stepped into the room and closed the door behind him, going over to the arm chair that didn't have the cardigan draped over it and sitting down. A large glass of brandy had been set on the table beside the chair—good brandy too, from the smell of it.

He stared at the glass for a long moment.

Alcohol was something he only touched sparingly these days, as he did with most of his old indulgences. He wasn't twenty any more and he had a country to run. His days of drinking in bars and partying in nightclubs were over.

Perhaps he should have asked Henri for some tea instead. Yet the chair was comfortable and he was tired, and the last couple of months discussing budgets and taxes had taken it out of him. Numbers weren't his thing. In fact, being a king in general wasn't his thing—he'd been brought up as the spare, not the heir—and it had taken him a good two years of hard work to get a decent grasp of what was expected of him.

Caspian should have been King, not you.

Yes, he should. But Caspian was dead and Cassius was all Aveiras had left.

The silence of the house settled around him like a balm. He was rarely alone these days. There were always people wanting something from him—a signature, an opinion, an order or even simply to be in his presence.

He found it tiring.

'Are you sure you don't want the crown, little brother?' Caspian had asked him one day. 'It's not too bad once you get used to carrying the weight of an entire country'.

Cassius had shuddered with distaste. 'I'll stick with carrying the weight of my own reputation, thank you very much. Which, luckily, is exceedingly light.'

He hadn't known then he'd end up stepping into his brother's shoes. Or that he'd end up carrying the weight of that crown, and all alone. But he hadn't had a choice, and he wouldn't let his family down—not again.

Cassius picked up the brandy glass and had already taken a few sips before being fully conscious of having done so. The alcohol sat warmly in his stomach, the taste rich and heavy on his tongue. He shouldn't indulge—control in all things was important—yet it seemed a shame to waste such a good vintage.

He only had time for a couple more sips before the library door opened suddenly and he looked up to find his wife standing in the doorway, staring at him.

It was late and he hadn't seen her all afternoon. She'd vanished after he'd finished sorting out the arrangements for himself and his staff for the night, and she hadn't been around when Henri had served dinner in the little dining room.

He'd made some enquiries as to her whereabouts, but Henri had only shaken his head and said he didn't know where Her Majesty was.

Cassius had told himself it didn't matter where she was, that he didn't care, but he couldn't shake the feeling that somehow he'd upset her.

She hadn't received the news of the divorce well. No matter that she'd told him she wasn't upset, he'd seen the shock in her eyes, and the hurt too.

She didn't look pleased to see him now, her pretty mouth firming as she spotted him sitting in the armchair.

She'd grown up into a lovely woman, which wasn't something he'd wanted to notice in his visits over the years, yet he'd noticed all the same. Once he'd been a connoisseur of women, and adult Inara was definitely a woman he'd have made time for.

If he'd still been the charming, feckless prince he'd once been, of course. But he wasn't. He had a duty to uphold, so he'd left that prince behind the moment he'd found out his family had died.

He hadn't taken a woman to his bed since and it wasn't because of a shortage of offers: he had more seduction attempts and frank invitations now he was a king than he'd ever had as a prince.

But his baser appetites had died along with the callow youth he'd once been, so he'd ignored every single offer. A king should be above reproach, as his father had always taught, an example of good leadership, and a new woman in his bed every night wasn't an example of good leadership.

Besides, as King he couldn't be seen to be unfaithful to his wife, even if they'd never consummated their marriage. Not that he'd found abstaining a hardship. Grief had killed any hint of the rebel in him and that was probably a good thing.

Yet he couldn't help noticing again that the

white cotton dress she wore was just as see-through now as it had been earlier that day, his attention drawn to the pink glow of pale skin and the lacy shadows of her underwear.

Something stirred inside him. Something he hadn't felt for a long time.

'Sorry,' Inara said stiffly. 'I didn't realise you were in here.'

He recalled that she wasn't a woman who hid her feelings and it was obvious that right now she was very annoyed. Hostile, even. He wasn't used to it from her and he found he didn't much like it.

'If I'm intruding you only need say,' he said formally.

'It's fine.' One small hand gripped the door handle. 'I'll leave you in peace—'

'Oh, come in,' he interrupted, feeling suddenly impatient, knowing he'd have to have this discussion with her at some point so he might as well have it now. 'We need to talk.'

'Do we?' She pushed her glasses up her nose with one finger. 'I think you said all you needed to earlier today.'

Cassius leaned forward, clasping his brandy

balloon between his fingers. He nodded at the chair opposite him. 'Sit.'

'I'm not one of your staff, Cassius. I don't appreciate being ordered around.'

He'd become used to people jumping every time he spoke. And maybe it was the brandy relaxing him but, instead of feeling irritated at her refusal, he was almost amused instead.

She hadn't been impressed with him even at sixteen, that night she'd appeared in his limo, even though he'd been a prince and she the under-age daughter of an unimportant family. She'd been suspicious of his marriage proposal, had asked a great many questions and had then insisted on him putting it in writing and signing it even before they'd got out of the limo.

It appeared she still wasn't impressed with him, even though he'd been King for three years.

'Please,' he added.

She wrinkled her nose, pursed that pretty mouth, finally let out a breath and let go of the door handle, coming over to the arm chair opposite and sitting down on the cardigan still half-draped over the seat.

'You're sitting on….' He gestured.

'Oh.' She frowned then wriggled half off the

seat, pulling the cardigan out from underneath her. 'Oh, there it is. I've been looking for that for ages.'

Watching her fuss with the cardigan was soothing, though he wasn't sure why. He took another sip of his brandy, his attention caught by the way she lifted the long, silvery waterfall of her hair off the nape of her neck so she could drape the cardigan around her. It was a deft, practised movement, her curls silky-looking as she shook her hair out over her shoulders.

She was still rather fairy-like, her features elfin and delicate, the shape of her slender and fragile.

She continued to fuss around with the cardigan, then adjusted her glasses, before smoothing her dress in small, agitated movements.

She's nervous...

He frowned. Why would she be nervous? Was it him? They'd known each other for five years and, although it was true he hadn't seen much of her the past couple of years, surely he was still familiar to her?

Or maybe it wasn't so much him as the topic of conversation: the divorce he'd asked for.

It mattered to her, as he'd already realised.

That was puzzling.

'Tell me,' he said after a moment. 'What's bothering you about this divorce?'

Her gaze dropped to her lap and she smoothed a non-existent crease in the fabric of her dress. 'Nothing. It was a shock, that's all.'

He didn't think that was all it was but, given how nervous she seemed, he decided not to press. 'And so you give me permission to start proceedings?'

'Do you need my permission?' She didn't look at him. 'You can do whatever you like. You're the King.'

'Yes, but you're still my wife.'

'No, I'm not. I might be your wife legally but I'm not in any other sense.'

Cassius watched her, caught by the strange, sharp note in her clear voice. If he hadn't known any better, he would have said that she sounded hurt, though he wasn't sure why that would be. Did she want to be more to him? If so, she must know how impossible that was. She was not in any way the Queen Aveiras needed and, as the country already had a king they hadn't asked for, he wasn't going to foist an unsuitable queen on them too.

That wasn't the legacy he wanted for the family he'd lost.

'That's true,' he said gently. 'So won't it be a relief to you when you're not my wife at all?'

She looked up, the colour of her eyes silvery behind her glasses. Idly, he noticed that her irises got darker closer to her pupils, the grey turning into charcoal. Her lashes were also darker, the contrast startling with her pale hair and skin.

'Why do you keep patronising me?' Her stare was very direct. 'You don't have to soothe me like a child. If you want to divorce me, divorce me. What does it matter if I agree to it or not?'

The feeling that had woken up inside him when she'd come in gripped him tighter. But he continued to ignore it, because he hadn't felt it for years, and he shouldn't be feeling it now, especially not with her.

Not when that way led back to the prince he'd once been and the choices he'd made that had changed his life for ever. He'd never be that prince, that careless man, again.

'I know you're not a child.' Absently, he cupped the brandy balloon between his palms, swirling the liquid, warming it. 'And I'm not trying to be patronising. I'm just trying to do the decent thing.'

She lifted one shoulder, her fingers pleating the fabric of her dress. 'Well, you don't need to.'

Cassius frowned. 'Would you really have preferred me to send a palace employee out with the divorce papers, then?'

'As long as you gave me some jewellery, that would have been fine.'

Ah, yes, the jewellery. He'd once been famous for showering his lovers with expensive pieces. He'd liked giving them gifts, small tokens of his appreciation for the pleasure they'd given him in return.

He'd thought himself so generous back then, but in reality once he'd got rid of a woman he'd never thought of her again. So, yes, he'd been generous with his money, but selfish and shallow with everything else.

It wasn't something he liked to be reminded of and he didn't like it now.

'Well, since I haven't actually slept with you,' he said, 'Jewellery wouldn't be appropriate.'

Her mouth opened then shut, and she blinked. 'Uh…no. That's true.'

You shouldn't have said that.

No. It had been inappropriate. Perhaps it was the brandy. In which case he should put down his glass and not have any more.

Except he didn't put down his glass. Instead he sat back in the comfortable arm chair and extended his legs, crossing them at the ankle. He took another sip.

He was relaxed, sitting here in the quiet of the house in this little room that was starting to feel more and more cosy despite the clutter. Relaxed in a way he hadn't felt for years. He knew he shouldn't be falling back into old habits, that he had a duty to his crown and to his country, but he wasn't in the vast, cold spaces of the royal palace in Katara now. He was here with Inara and there was no one to see him but her.

'What exactly is the issue, Inara?' he asked after a moment. 'You keep telling me that nothing's wrong yet any fool can see that something is.'

She didn't respond, merely continued pleating the fabric of her dress and smoothing it out.

'You're…interrupting my research,' she said at last.

'Your research.' More amusement coiled inside him. 'And how exactly am I interrupting it?'

'Oh, just by being…' She made a vague gesture in his direction. 'Here. In the house. Hovering.'

He grinned, unable to help himself. 'Hovering?'

She wriggled her fingers. 'Yes, you know. Just by being around and being…distracting.'

That amused him too. 'I'm distracting?'

A wash of delicate pink swept through her cheeks. 'It's not funny.'

Unaccountably fascinated, Cassius stared. The pink accentuated the grey of her eyes and gave her the most pretty glow. He had a sudden vision of what she'd look like if there had been a fire in the fireplace and the warm light of it was flickering over her. If she was naked, without all that white cotton in the way, just her silvery hair flowing over her shoulders and her pale skin pink and bare. He'd pull her from that chair, lay her down on the rug before the fire, spread her thighs and kneel between them. And then he'd…

What the hell are you thinking that for?

Cassius took a sharp breath. He shouldn't be thinking such things, and especially not about Inara. She wasn't the sixteen-year-old he'd married, it was true, but he couldn't afford to start thinking of her as anything else.

She was young and innocent, and her place was in some university somewhere, putting that genius brain of hers to work. He was going to divorce her and find another woman more suitable to be his wife. A mature, self-contained woman who comported herself with dignity and who could give Aveiras the heirs it needed.

And, apart from anything else, the whole reason he'd married her was to save her from one selfish monster, not put her in danger from another. And most especially if that monster was himself.

But Inara is here right now and she's your wife...

Unfamiliar heat wound through him, intense and raw. It had been so long since he'd been with a woman, run his fingers through her hair, touched her silky skin. So long since soft thighs had closed around his waist and tight, wet heat had brought him home. So long since he'd had kisses and hot whispers in his ear... So very, *very* long...

Cassius became aware that Inara was watching him and that her cheeks had gone an even deeper shade of pink. Something in her eyes glinted and he could feel a certain tension gathering in the space between them.

A tension that hadn't been there before and yet was familiar. He'd felt it with other women, years ago, though it had never been quite as... electric as this.

'Of course it's not funny.' His voice was thicker than he would have liked. 'You should leave. I'm not fit company for anyone tonight.'

Inara stared at him for a long moment, then slowly shook her head. 'No,' she said. 'I don't think I will.'

CHAPTER THREE

SOMETHING WAS TELLING Inara that she should do exactly what he'd said and leave, yet another part of her kept whispering that she should stay. That it had been a long time since she'd seen him like this, all stretched out, long and lean and as muscular as a panther half-asleep in the sun.

When she'd been younger, in the first couple of years after they'd married, he'd set her up in a house in Katara, with Henri and Joan to run the place and keep an eye on her. She'd been ignored by the King and Queen, Cassius's parents, because they had strongly disapproved of Cassius marrying her, but that hadn't mattered to Inara. She was used to parental disapproval, and besides, being safe from her own parents' plans had been more important than anything else.

Cassius had been a regular visitor back then. They'd have dinner together before he'd go out to a club or a party or some royal function. He'd been funny and charming and interested in what she'd had to say. His eyes hadn't glazed over when she'd talked about her mathematical studies and he hadn't scoffed at her enthusiasm or forbidden her to talk about it, the way her parents had done. He hadn't picked at how she looked, or criticised everything she did, or talked about her while she was in the room as if she weren't there.

She'd always found talking to people in social situations difficult, but nothing was difficult about being with him, and she wasn't sure why. Maybe it was simply that he was the first person who'd actually seemed to listen to her. Whatever, his visits had made her happy.

But that had been before Prince Caspian and the King and Queen had died, and Cassius had ascended to the throne.

After that, he'd changed.

He'd become distant, colder, more rigid. He didn't smile or laugh, and soon enough he didn't visit much either. It had been like watching a flesh-and-blood man turn slowly into stone and she'd been powerless to stop it.

She wasn't sure if this happened to every man when they became a king, or whether it was just him, but the one thing she was sure of was that she hated it.

Except he didn't look like stone now. He was sitting sprawled out in her favourite arm chair, the one large enough for her to curl up in and roomy enough to accommodate his broad shoulders and powerful chest with ease. The cold distance she'd always felt in him had receded and the line of his stern mouth was relaxed, as if he might at any moment give her the warm, effortlessly charming smile she'd fallen in love with.

In fact, every line of him seemed relaxed, as if he were a soldier who'd taken off his suit of armour after a hard day's battle.

She didn't want to move or even breathe in case something changed and he turned back into stone again.

He tilted his head, studying her from underneath thick, black lashes, a strange, glimmering heat in the smoky amber of his gaze.

It reminded her of him in the limo all those years ago, sprawled just like this, all coiled, muscled strength and devastating masculine charm, with his pick of the women standing at the kerb, waiting to be his chosen partner for the evening. She hadn't taken much notice of them that night—she'd been too busy being scared, yet determined to go through with her own plan—but she did remember wondering why they'd all looked so flushed and excited.

She knew the reason now, and she knew why they had been desperate, and she wished suddenly that she'd been one of them. That she'd had the chance to be his chosen lover for the evening.

Well, why can't you be?

The thought came like a light switching on in a dark room, illuminating everything, and she had to blink a couple of times to get used to the glare.

'That's probably a mistake.' His voice had deepened, the timbre of it warm, soft and velvety. 'I'm not feeling kind tonight.'

Inara barely took in what he'd said, too busy examining the new and quite frankly exciting idea that had sprung to glaring prominence in her head.

Why *couldn't* she be his lover for the night? True, he'd never shown an interest in her but, as he kept saying, that was because he still saw her as the sixteen-year-old girl who'd slipped into his limo.

She'd told him she wasn't sixteen any more, but he hadn't seemed to listen. Like everyone in her life while she'd been growing up...

Annoyance twisted inside her, along with a new determination. Perhaps she needed to be more obvious. Perhaps he needed to *see* that she wasn't a teenager any more. Perhaps she needed to prove it to him. And perhaps, if she did that, he might actually see her differently. He might...want her.

Her heart was beating very fast and her mouth had gone dry. She knew how to work out complicated algebraic equations, but she didn't have the first clue how to go about making him see her as a woman.

'I don't need you to be kind,' she said distractedly, her brain too occupied with sorting through plans and discarding them. What was the best way to go about this? Where did she start? What did other women do in this situation?

More than once she'd spent whole evenings on her computer, searching for anything she could find on him—scrolling through endless articles and gossip columns, studying the photos of him and the women he had on his arm. Sometimes they'd been drop-dead gorgeous, and sometimes they hadn't been conventionally beautiful, but they'd all seemed to have…something that had drawn him to them. She'd wondered what that something was and had concluded it wasn't something she'd ever have.

But was that actually the case? She was a mathematician, and all good equations needed to be proved. This was exactly the same. If she had conclusive proof that he didn't want her, then it would hurt, but she could accept that. She could accept the divorce too. But if he did want her…

Maybe you could make him change his mind about the divorce.

Inara swallowed. A strange tension filled the room that hadn't been there before. It prickled over her skin, made her breathing get faster.

'What are you thinking about?' Cassius asked. 'It's obviously very important.

Inara forced herself to look up from the mess she'd made of her dress. He was watching her in a very focussed, intent way, his long fingers cradling his brandy glass, swirling the liquid in it idly.

She was often guilty of over-thinking things— that came with the territory of having an anxious, over-excited brain—but maybe it was best if she didn't over-think this particular thing. Maybe she just needed to…act. Do what her instinct told her for a change.

She hadn't had any experience with that, as her instincts had always been wrong in the past—at least, that was what her parents had said—but right now she had nothing to lose. Tomorrow he'd be leaving for Katara and the palace, and her one chance to get him to see her differently, to change his mind, would be gone.

It was now or never.

So she didn't think, just pushed herself up and out of her chair, moving over to where he sat.

He arched one dark brow. 'What do you want, little one?'

'I'm not that little.' She stopped in front of his chair, considering her next move.

'No,' he murmured. 'Perhaps you're not.' His gaze travelled over her in a leisurely fashion and it felt almost as if he was looking right through the material of her dress…

Inara's skin prickled with sudden heat, her breath catching.

He *was* doing that, wasn't he? Because, come to think of it, her dress was a little see-through—

not that she'd ever paid much attention, as for the past five years she hadn't had to worry about her appearance.

But now that heat was in his eyes, glowing like banked embers, and she could feel the pressure of his stare like a hand stroking slowly over her skin, she suddenly wanted more than anything in the entire world to be beautiful for him. To be sexy and desirable, to be his choice for the night. Not the scared sixteen-year-old her own parents had been willing to give to a monster.

She took a slow breath, then another, trying to control the frantic beat of her heart. Then she took a couple of steps closer until she was standing almost next to the chair. His legs were outstretched in front of him, crossed at the ankle, and she was painfully aware of how long and powerful he was. So much bigger than she was and so much stronger.

She wasn't sure why that made her so breathless, but then that was the problem with Cassius. Everything about him made her breathless.

His head rested against the back of the chair, his eyes gleaming as he looked up at her, the tension between them pulling tighter.

Say something, idiot.

'Um, I've never had brandy before,' she said, her voice scratchy. 'Can I have a taste?'

He shifted slightly and she found her attention flickering to his body once again. She noted the stretch of his trousers over his powerful thighs and the pull of the cotton over his shoulders. He'd got rid of his jacket and tie, and his shirt was unbuttoned at the throat. She could see his pulse beating beneath smooth olive skin, strong and steady...

'Never?' he asked.

There was a look in his eyes and a certain hot note in his voice that made her think he wasn't just talking about brandy. But she wasn't sure what else he could be talking about. Whatever it was, she was suddenly hotter and even more breathless than before.

'No.' She didn't know what to do with her hands except clasp them in front of her. 'Is it nice?'

Inwardly, part of her cringed. She sounded so silly. Like a little girl. But what else could she say? Social graces and small talk had never come easily to her, much to her mother's annoyance, and as for getting the attention of a man, well...

'For God's sake, Inara,' her mother had said at the first aristocratic gathering to which they'd managed to swing an invite. 'If you can't open your mouth without boring everyone to tears, then just shut it and smile. Some men like a quiet woman.'

So she'd been quiet after that, as she couldn't trust herself to say anything interesting. And clearly she shouldn't trust herself now, especially when he'd be used to all kinds of beautiful, experienced women. Women who were far more interesting than she was, and far more beautiful too. Not pale and weedy and weak-looking. Untidy and chaotic and awkward, hardly anyone's prize.

Except he's looking at you like you might be his.

And he was. Or at least she thought he was. The smoky amber of his gaze was now a hot golden-brown, like the warmed brandy in his glass, and there was something distinctly speculative in it. As if he was imagining things…

Her palms were sweaty and she couldn't breathe, and part of her wanted to turn around and leave the room, flee back to the safety of her study or her bedroom, or basically anywhere he wasn't.

'Being good at maths is useless to us, Inara,' her mother had said coldly after the last social failure. 'We need an aristocratic alliance and if you can't even manage that then what good are you?'

Good enough to turn over to an old man who had an unhealthy obsession with young girls, apparently.

But she wasn't her parents' chess piece now and she'd had five years of freedom from being criticised constantly. And, more than anything else, if she didn't follow through with this she knew she'd never find out what it would be like to be wanted by him. To be touched by him. To have a night with him…

She'd never have a chance to change his mind about divorcing her, and she'd never have something of him to keep for herself if that didn't work.

So she stayed where she was, breathless and aching, and afraid and excited all at the same time.

His mouth curved in a faint, lazy smile. 'Yes. It's very nice. Come here and you can have a taste.' He uncrossed his feet and spread his thighs, indicating that she was to come and stand between them.

The aching, breathless feeling inside her intensified.

Slowly, she moved to stand in front of his chair, between those powerful thighs, while he gazed at her, golden-brown eyes gleaming under silky black lashes.

It was strange to have him look up at her when normally she was the one looking up. Even so, she felt his power. Even when she was sitting down the impact of his presence made her want to go on her knees before him.

Cassius sat forward. 'Here,' he said softly. 'Take a sip.' And he extended his hand, holding his glass out to her.

Her heartbeat was louder now and she could feel the heat coming off him, making the fierce longing inside her tighten.

Whenever she thought about getting close to him, her fantasies were always veiled and gauzy. Kisses, certainly, though she had no idea what a kiss felt like or tasted like. She definitely imagined his arms around her, holding her, and sometimes in the dead of night she imagined his hands on her.

But those were furtive imaginings, making her restless and hot, vaguely feverish and a little afraid, so she tried not to imagine that too much.

It wasn't that she didn't know about sex. It was more that thinking about it in terms of herself and Cassius was too much. The depth of her own feeling about it was too much.

But now she was closer to him than she'd ever been in her life and it wasn't like her teenage imaginings. It was more immediate, more physical, more visceral than those gauzy fantasies had ever been.

Inara swallowed and put her hand out for the glass, only for him to pull it back slightly and out of her reach. How annoying. She took a tiny step closer, reaching out again, only for him to do the same thing.

He watched her, his mouth curving, his gaze full of what looked like challenge mixed with something hot and wicked. A tease.

He was doing this on purpose, wasn't he?

Of course he is. He's flirting with you.

What little breath she had left caught in her throat, a strange euphoria sweeping through her.

Because, while she didn't know much of anything about flirting, a very female part of her told her that was what he was doing. Which could only mean one thing: he saw her not just as a woman, but as a woman he was attracted to. A woman he wanted.

'What are you doing?' she asked huskily, wanting to be sure.

'I think you know what I'm doing.' That devastatingly sexy smile deepened, his eyes gleaming. 'If you want a taste of my brandy, little one, you're going to have to come much closer than that.'

Cassius knew he was being grossly inappropriate. But the brandy had gone to his head, he was tired and it had been a long time since he'd allowed himself to enjoy the company of a pretty woman. A long time since he'd flirted with anyone. A long time since he'd felt desire at all.

Yet desire was coiling through him now, and even though she was the wrong woman to be feeling this about, the wrong woman to be using his old flirting skills on, he couldn't bring himself to stop.

She was just so…pretty. And sweet. And so

very innocent, in her white dress with her mismatched underwear plainly visible underneath. She was also very slender and fragile, her eyes silvery from behind the lenses of her glasses, her hair lying loose over her shoulders like moonlight.

His child bride.

Except she wasn't a child any more. Her cheeks had gone pink and she was looking at him in a way that was intimately familiar to him. He'd seen it before in the faces of too many women to count.

She wanted him.

He hadn't expected that, though in retrospect he should have, and it was a warning sign that he needed to stop. Because nothing could happen between them. Nothing *should* happen between them, not when they were going to separate. Their marriage needed to stay unconsummated, because she was so much younger than him, and because he wasn't the man he'd once been—that reckless playboy with no purpose in life but to indulge his own selfish needs. He was trying to put distance between himself and that man, and seducing his lovely, innocent wife was definitely *not* putting distance between them.

Also, it wasn't what his parents would have wanted. They'd been appalled at his marriage, never mind that he'd done it to save Inara, and they'd certainly be appalled at what he was contemplating now. Then again, his parents had been dead for three years, and he was so tired of being good. Tired of being rigid and distant and controlled. Tired of having to set an example. Tired of being the King.

Would it be so wrong to have one night where he could indulge himself? To sip a good brandy and flirt with a pretty woman? That was all—just flirt. He wouldn't take it any further. But he could have that, couldn't he?

A crease had appeared between Inara's brows, as if she was contemplating doing what he'd said and getting closer to him, and he found himself breathless at the thought that she might.

It was not an unreasonable response. It had been years since he'd allowed a woman to get close, so it probably had more to do with her being female than it did with Inara herself.

Anyway, he wanted to know what she smelled like. Did she wear perfume? He didn't think she would. There was no artifice to her; everything about her was haphazard and untidy. But also very, very honest.

She wasn't trying to be anyone other than who she was.

Unlike you.

Ah, but he couldn't be who he was. Being a king demanded that he be more than a mere man. Something greater and more noble, more just. The ultimate in selflessness and self-sacrifice.

Cassius's father had been the model he'd tried to emulate—compassionate yet distant. Protective yet controlled. A great king, everyone had said.

What would they all think of you now? Letting the brandy go to your head while you flirt with the wife you swore you'd never touch...

The thought came and went, and Cassius let it go. Because Inara took another step. The white cotton of her dress brushed against his trousers as she leaned down, reaching for the brandy glass in his hand.

But she wasn't looking at the glass.

She was looking at him.

He lifted the glass before she could take it and sipped some of the brandy, and then, before she had a chance to straighten, he slipped a hand around the back of her neck and brought her mouth down on his.

It was a reflex, an instinct he thought he'd long since left behind, and he knew even as he reached for her that it was wrong. But he didn't stop. And when that perfect rosebud of a mouth touched his he didn't want to stop.

Her lips were soft beneath his and he could feel the muscles in the back of her neck tense, her body going very still. Her shock was palpable, but she didn't pull away. And when he opened his mouth, letting her take a sip of the brandy directly from him, she gave a little moan.

He was right, though; she wore no perfume. Her scent was a combination of laundry powder, something flowery that must be either shampoo or soap, and a sweet, warm, musky scent that had to be intrinsic to her.

It was so unexpectedly erotic that he increased the pressure on the back of her neck, trying to draw her in closer, before he'd even thought about it. She didn't protest, the soft lips beneath his opening, her tongue shyly seeking his. Inexpert yet hungry, and clearly wanting more.

You fool. What are you doing?

He didn't know but, whatever it was, it had to stop.

Cassius sat back, releasing his hold on her, trying to draw away as he put his brandy glass on the table beside his chair. But Inara wouldn't let him. She slid her arms around his neck, leaning into him, her knees pressing against the seat of his chair. Her kiss was hungrier, her mouth hot, sweet and alcoholic, going straight to his head as surely as the brandy had.

It had been so long since he'd kissed a woman. He'd forgotten how good it felt to have a soft mouth on his and warm arms around him.

It made him hungry. So hungry.

Without thought, Cassius settled his hands on her hips and pulled her down into his lap, positioning her so she knelt on the seat astride him. She sighed, winding her arms around his neck and pressing herself delicately against him, kissing him harder, her inexperience clear, yet still so hungry for him.

It set him on fire.

The erotic scent of her skin was everywhere, the heavy silk of her hair falling like a curtain around him. He lifted his hands to it, buried his fingers in its softness and closed them into fists, holding on tight. Her arms tightened around his neck.

The heat of her mouth stole everything from him, his breath, his resistance, his common sense. It put down the King and coaxed out the man instead. The man he hadn't been in years.

Desire rushed through him like a tide, relentless, unstoppable, and before he knew what he was doing he'd unwound his fingers from her hair and was tugging at the hem of her dress, pushing it up around her hips.

She made another of those delicious, sexy, throaty sounds and, when his hands slid up her bare thighs, her skin warm and silky, she quivered. So responsive. She was everything he'd been missing and more. All the blood in his body rushed south, concentrating itself behind his fly. He was so hard, he hurt.

Her skin beneath his fingers felt hot, and when he slipped his hand between her thighs, stroking her through the lacy fabric of her knickers, she felt even hotter. She shuddered as he touched her and he could feel wetness against his fingertips.

Dear God, he couldn't think.

He curled his fingers into the material and pulled it roughly aside so he could touch her more directly. She was hot and wet, and when he found the delicate bud hidden in the slick folds of her sex she cried out against his mouth, her hips shuddering under his hand.

Beautiful, sexy little woman.

'I want you,' he said roughly. 'I want you here. Now. So if you don't want it too, you'd better tell me immediately.'

'I do.' Her voice was breathless and frayed. 'I want you, Cassius. Oh, please… *Please…*'

The need inside him was too big, too demanding. He couldn't deny it even if he'd wanted to. But he didn't want to. The world had narrowed down to the slick feel of her sex, the sweet musk of her skin and the rich, heady taste of her mouth.

For three years he'd had nothing but cold, echoing palace rooms, the sense of being constantly surrounded by people, yet always feeling alone. The iron control he had to maintain over himself all the time, and the hard edges of difficult decisions. The sharp thorns of grief and guilt.

But here in his hands was softness and warmth and pleasure. The chance to lose himself, to feel something other than those terrible, difficult emotions. The chance to feel something good.

So he took it.

He reached for the button on his trousers, undid it, then pulled down the zip. He pushed aside the fabric and freed himself, positioning her over him. Then he pulled her down onto him as he thrust up.

She cried out, her back arching, her body shuddering.

She was so tight, he could barely get a breath.

He wound his fingers into her hair and pulled back, looking up into her delicate face. Her cheeks were flushed a deep pink, the lenses of her glasses foggy, and she was looking at him in shock.

'Are you with me?' he demanded. 'I'm sorry. I can't be slow and I can't be gentle.'

She blinked a couple of times and then suddenly she was kissing him again and her body was softening around him, gripping him tight, the heat of her astonishing. Clearly, she was with him.

He couldn't hold himself back. His hands settled on her hips once more and he began to move her on him, fast and deep, because it couldn't be anything else for him, not right now. There was nothing in him but need. Nothing in the whole world he wanted right now but her.

He kissed her back, taking control, tasting her, feasting on her, his hips flexing, thrusting into the wet heat of her body. She denied him nothing, her own kisses hungry, pressing herself even closer, trying to match the movement of his hips with hers.

In some dim, forgotten part of his brain, a judgmental piece of himself was shouting at him to stop. That she was inexperienced, a virgin, the bride he'd married when she'd been sixteen and that he should not be doing this to her. That at the very least he should be gentle and careful and patient.

But there was no time to show her what to do and he had no patience left. He put a hand between her thighs once more, finding that sensitive little bundle of nerves, stroking her with firm, definite movements until she gave a soft, sobbing cry, her body convulsing around his.

Then he was moving deep and hard, single-mindedly chasing his own pleasure until it exploded like a glory around him and he was lost in the heart of it, forgetting for the first time in three years that he was a king.

CHAPTER FOUR

INARA LAY SLUMPED against Cassius's broad chest, her head resting on his shoulder, her heart feeling as if it were trying to batter its way out of her chest. The muscles of her inner thighs hurt, the delicate skin between them was burning and her mouth felt full, sensitive and a touch bruised.

She couldn't see past the foggy lenses of her glasses and the frames were askew on her face, one of the arms having come loose from her ear. Small electric shocks of pleasure continued to pulse inside her. She felt dazed, shocked, astonished and completely unable to move.

Cassius's rapidly slowing heartbeat was in her ear, his warm breath stirring her hair. His body felt hard and huge beneath her, as if she were lying on a slab of warm granite, and the familiar scent of his aftershave—sandalwood and spice—surrounded her.

She couldn't believe what had just happened. It had been...amazing. Shocking. Exciting. Incredible. Though, really, none of those words even came close to encompassing the entire experience that was sex with Cassius de Leon.

She hadn't expected that kiss, his mouth hot and firm, and then the taste of brandy on her lips. The heat of the alcohol had somehow got inside her, made her even hungrier and thirstier, and all her uncertainty and doubt had dropped away.

He'd kissed her and it had been unlike anything she'd ever experienced in her entire life. Better than those gauzy fantasies. More intense and more real, and somehow more confronting too. But so, *so* good.

And then his hands on her, touching her. Authoritative and demanding. And the pleasure that had followed in its wake...

It had been an intensely physical experience which was quite new to her. She existed so much of the time in her head, often forgetting her own bodily needs, that this had been...well...frankly overwhelming.

She'd never been so aware of physical sensation before, of her own skin and his hands on it. Of the need inside her, pleasure winding tighter and tighter, taking her out of her head and grounding her firmly in her body. She hadn't known it would feel like that, that she'd like it and that she'd want more, so much more.

He shifted, withdrawing from her and causing her to shiver helplessly in reaction. That moment he'd thrust inside her had been a shock, even though she'd been expecting it. There had been a sharp pain and a burning sensation, and the weird, suffocating feeling of having someone else inside her body.

But then that had all fallen away, leaving behind it an intense, dragging ache that had become more and more acute as he'd moved inside her.

She'd wanted to hold onto it, keep it going for as long as possible, but then his hand had slipped between her thighs, finding that exquisitely sensitive part of her and stroking her, making the pleasure fold in on itself, layering it until it had burst apart like a firework.

Inara let out a shaky breath, the memory making her shiver yet again.

But then his hands were adjusting her, smoothing down her dress, and she wasn't sure what that meant. Were they done? Was that all sex was? She didn't know much about it, but she was pretty sure there was more to it than that, surely?

'Cassius,' she began in a croaky voice.

He ignored her, holding out the brandy glass. 'Here. You might need this.' His face was expressionless, though the gold in his eyes glowed hot with the remains of desire.

She didn't want to move. She liked lying against him, but the blank look on his face chilled her. It didn't seem as if what they'd done together had been as amazing and incredible for him as it had been for her.

What did you expect? That you were special?

The chill creeping through her widened. She hadn't thought about it. She hadn't expected him to be here at all, let alone to have sex with him in a chair in the library. But now she *was* thinking about it... Yes, of course she wanted to be special, because he was special to her.

Except that clearly wasn't the case. The wicked amusement that had curved his mouth and the sensual challenge in his eyes from before had disappeared. The lines of his face were set, his gaze veiled by his long black lashes. She was still in his lap, resting against his chest, surrounded by his heat, but she had the sense that he was slipping away from her. That the warm, wicked, teasing man she'd first met in the limo, who'd visited her many times over the years, was gone again.

It was the King she was looking at now.

And maybe, for the King, she was just another in a long line of women he slept with, because she had no doubt he slept with other women. His fidelity or otherwise was something she'd never thought about, as their marriage wasn't a real marriage.

But she didn't like the thought of it now. Specifically, she didn't like the thought of being just another woman he took to his bed. The warmth and pleasure from the orgasm drained away, leaving her feeling cold and empty, so she sat up and took the glass from him, sipping the brandy in an effort to warm herself up.

He watched her, his gaze impersonal. 'Are you all right?' His voice was very deep and she could hear a slight roughness in it. 'Did I hurt you in any way?'

The questions sounded impersonal too; the only thing giving away what they'd done together was the rough note in his voice.

Inara's throat tightened despite the brandy.

'I'm fine,' she forced out. 'And, no, you didn't hurt me.'

'Good.' He studied her, frowning, then took the brandy glass away from her before she could have another sip.

She stared at him. 'I hadn't finished.'

He ignored that. 'You were a virgin, weren't you?'

'Well...yes.' It seemed a strange question to ask, especially given how young she'd been when they'd married. 'I was only sixteen when you married me.'

'But you're twenty-one now, correct?'

'Yes.'

'And you haven't been seeing anyone?'

Inara blinked, the thought so foreign to her she didn't take it in at first. The idea that she would even look at anyone else was inconceivable.

'No,' she said, astonished at the question. 'Why would I?'

He didn't answer. He glanced away, a line between his black brows making it clear he was thinking hard about something.

She didn't understand what was going on. She wasn't sure what was supposed to happen after sex, but it couldn't be questions about her virginity, with him frowning and not even looking at her? There had been romantic movies... She'd watched as the couple had held each other and kissed after sex, or had deep and meaningful conversations. It hadn't been...this.

Perhaps trying to seduce him had been a mistake. Perhaps she'd done it wrong, because she often got things wrong, or so her mother used to tell her.

You're so naive. You think you know what you're doing and you don't. You have no idea...

The need to get away, to put some distance between them, gripped her and she struggled to sit up, pushing at the hard plane of his chest.

'Don't,' he murmured, his arms tightening.

'Why?' Her heartbeat had picked up speed again, the chill winding through her intensifying. It hurt to be here in his arms, to feel as if she'd made a mistake, a terrible mistake. 'Let me go, Cassius.'

'No.' His arms held her captive and when he looked down at her she could see heat still in his eyes, glowing like embers. 'Be still.'

'Why?' She shoved at him again. 'What do you want from me? If I'm just another woman to you—'

'What do you mean just another woman?'

She took a breath, her heartbeat thudding hard in her ears. He was frowning ferociously at her as if she'd said something hugely offensive. 'Well, clearly I've done something you didn't like, because you went all cold and distant. I don't know what your other lovers—'

'I don't have any other lovers,' he interrupted flatly. 'There's just you, Inara.'

No, that couldn't be right. He was the King. He could have any woman he wanted, and he must have wanted quite a few. His reputation as a lover had been widespread and notorious, and she'd assumed that he would have carried on in the same vein.

But…apparently not.

'What?' She stared at him in shock. 'What do you mean, just me?'

An expression she didn't understand flickered over his face. Then it vanished and the same calm mask he always wore descended once more.

'I mean exactly what I said.' His voice was very level. 'I haven't had a lover in three years.'

Inara's shock deepened. If he hadn't had a lover in three years then that meant…well…that he'd been celibate. Which for an ex-playboy was unthinkable.

His calm mask rippled—the mask of a king… she could see that now—then settled. 'Yes, you might well look at me like that. A faithful husband isn't exactly what you expected of me, is it?'

There didn't seem to be any bitterness in his tone yet she caught echoes of it all the same. She didn't understand. She hadn't asked for a faithful husband—she hadn't been thinking of sex at sixteen, and he'd been adamant he wasn't going to touch her. That he wasn't going to tell her what to do or demand things of her. It was only a legal marriage, he'd said. A signature on a piece of paper, nothing more.

And, even when she'd begun to realise that her feelings for him were not those she should have for the kindly uncle he'd told her to think of him as, she hadn't given one single thought to all the women he seduced and spent time with.

You put him on a pedestal and kept him there.

The thought was unexpected, and all the more so because as soon as it had occurred to her she knew it was true. She *had* put him on a pedestal. She hadn't thought of him as an uncle, but she hadn't thought of him as a man either. He'd been a handsome, charming playboy prince, and then a distant, almost mythical king.

Except he wasn't that prince any longer and, as she'd just found out, he wasn't solely a king either. He was a man too. A human being. A person she knew nothing about.

Something kicked hard in her brain. Curiosity.

'I never thought of you as a husband at all,' she said before she could think better of it. 'But why? Have you really been celibate for three years?'

'Yes.' This time there was no hesitation. 'I have a standard to uphold and it's a standard I believe in very much. A king has to set an example to his people, so that's what I strive to do. They expect their king to behave in a certain way, and sleeping around is not one of those behaviours.'

The chill that had crept through her just before was back, though she wasn't sure why, not when what he'd said made sense. The de Leon kings had always been exemplary in their behaviour, shining lights of compassion and justice and propriety. Certainly, Cassius's father had been a perfect example, and his twin brother

Caspian a carbon copy. It made sense that Cassius would now take on that mantle.

So why did he break a three-year drought with you?

She had no idea. Desperation? Opportunity? Certainly it wasn't because she was special in any way.

'So why now?' she couldn't help asking. 'Why did you…?'

Cassius cupped her jaw gently, his touch silencing her. Glimmers of heat still shone in his eyes, but she could tell the King was very firmly in charge now. 'Because you were lovely and I forgot myself.' His gaze was very direct. 'But now we have an added difficulty. I didn't use a condom.'

Oh. She hadn't even thought of that.

Her stomach dropped away and she felt slightly dizzy at the idea that she might be expecting Cassius's child.

'It's not ideal for either of us,' he went on, his thumb absently stroking her cheek, 'but there is only one way we can solve this.'

'Solve this?' she echoed, her thoughts tumbling around in her head, her skin burning with every stroke of his thumb.

'Yes, of course. It's a problem, Inara.' His hand dropped away. 'But it's a problem that I created and therefore I will be the one to find a solution.'

Her brain felt sluggish, all her thought processes sticky as treacle. 'A solution to what?'

'To the fact that I took your virginity,' he said patiently. 'To the fact that you might be expecting my heir. Don't you see? A divorce is out of the question now.'

Inara was warm and soft and delicate against him, and her eyes had gone very wide, staring at him in shock.

Well, he could understand that. This was shocking for him too. He'd lost control. He'd forgotten himself. He'd taken her without thought, without consideration, and most important of all without a condom.

He was appalled at himself. He was supposed to be better than this. Hadn't he promised himself that? He was supposed to protect her, to be her saviour, not her ravisher. After his parents' and Caspian's deaths, he'd sworn that he'd be the kind of king they'd have been proud of. He'd never be Caspian, of course—who could?—but he'd at least be decent.

A decent king wouldn't take the virginity of a woman as innocent as Inara.

A decent king wouldn't forget a damn condom either.

Which meant that, if he wanted to be a decent king, the only answer was to keep her as his wife.

'What?' She blinked rapidly. 'You don't want a divorce? But I thought you said—'

'I know what I said,' he interrupted, ignoring the regret and bitter shame coiling in his heart. Regret over what this would mean for Inara. Shame at how easily he'd forgotten his vows to himself and his family. 'But things have changed. If you're pregnant with my heir, there will be no divorce.'

It was the only solution. No, she wouldn't be who he'd have chosen as his queen—his parents would have been horrified—but there wasn't another fix. He could divorce her, but what if she was pregnant? He couldn't have a royal bastard running around. That just wouldn't work.

And if she wasn't pregnant, he'd still taken her virginity. No one else would know, but *he* would. He'd know exactly how thin were his promises, how fragile. And, if he couldn't even keep a promise to himself, how could he keep it to anyone else? To his country?

No, he couldn't countenance it. He wouldn't.

'But I…might not be pregnant.'

'You might not,' he agreed. 'But the fact remains that I took your virginity. And, besides, you're my wife already. Seems logical that you should stay my wife.'

'But I—'

'Don't worry.' Gently, he lifted the arm of her glasses that had come off and slipped it back behind her ear. Perhaps she would be more comfortable with contacts. They might be easier to manage, given that as Queen she'd be attending functions and undertaking numerous other royal duties. 'I'll handle everything. It'll be an adjustment for you being Queen, as it was for me when I became King, but I managed well enough. And so will you.'

'Queen?' she repeated faintly. 'But I don't want… I mean, not officially…'

She'd gone very pale, looking even more ethereal than she normally did, and the shame and regret inside him sunk deeper.

If he needed another reason why this had been a mistake, then here it was. Just as he'd never

expected to be King, Inara had never expected
to be Queen in anything but name. He'd automatically undertaken most of the official duties
on his own, because he'd sensed her discomfort
with the role, leaving her safe to pursue her own
interests here at the Queen's Estate.

He knew she hated the palace in Katara. She
hated being looked at and talked about. Hated
the social engagements that being a queen involved, the functions and parties and balls and
openings she'd be expected to attend. She hated
being the object of everyone's attention and, as
he could do most of that himself, he'd left her
to her own devices.

Choosing another woman to do that duty had
seemed like a kindness, so her arguing about
it earlier had made no sense. Unless of course
she'd changed her mind. Now, though, it was obvious she hadn't changed her mind. She clearly
regarded being queen as similar to going to her
doom.

*She'll have to learn how to deal with it. As
you did.*

Cassius wasn't a cruel man. There was no
profit in it, and besides, a king should never be
cruel, although sometimes justice could look

like cruelty. And sometimes doing the right thing could look the same way.

It probably looked that way to her now.

'I know you don't.' He gave her what he hoped was an understanding look. 'But there are times when we don't get to choose. And this is one of those times.'

'Cassius…'

He put a gentle finger over her mouth, silencing her. 'That's my decision, little one.' Her lips were very soft, very warm, and suddenly all he could think about was how they'd felt beneath his and how she'd tasted of brandy and desire and every good thing…

If you stay here, you'll risk making the same mistake again.

It was true. He could already feel his body begin to harden once more, responding to her soft weight in his arms and her sweet scent, the delicate curves of her body pressing against him.

He could have her again. He could take her upstairs and spend the night with her. It wouldn't make any difference to his decision and, if he was going to keep her as his wife, then it would be a marriage in all senses of the word. There would be no celibacy for him any more.

But, although it was tempting, he needed to get some distance between himself and the appalling mistake he'd made. Some time to recall his own promises and put in place safeguards to make sure he wouldn't lose himself so completely again.

She'd need some time to come to terms with what he'd told her too, and what it would mean. And there'd definitely have to be a period of adjustment. Which meant that sitting here with her in his lap was probably not a good idea.

Carefully, Cassius shifted her off him, getting up from the chair then settling her back into it. She looked up at him, small and, fragile and wide-eyed, curled up on the big leather seat.

'So…that's it?' Inara said. 'I don't get a say in this?'

'As I said, sometimes we don't get to choose our path in life, and this is one of those times.' He checked his watch, impatience gathering in him. Normally he'd ignore it, as impatience was not an admirable quality in a ruler, but right now he had a few things to do. There were arrangements to be made and certain things to be put in place if he was going to bring Inara back to the palace, which he would. As soon as possible.

'But you didn't want me to be your queen. You wanted someone else. You said I wasn't a suitable choice.'

There was a desperate note in her voice that made his chest tighten, though he wasn't sure why she was trying to argue with him now, when she had seemed so opposed to the divorce only a few hours ago.

'You're not. But I don't have a choice about this either.' He tried not to let his own regret and impatience show, given it was clear she needed some reassurance, and him getting angry wouldn't help. Especially as it wasn't her fault. The blame lay entirely with him. 'Don't worry, Inara,' he went on in softer tones. 'I'll do all I can to ensure that you'll be the best queen Aveiras can hope for.'

She said nothing, her face white, her eyes going dark behind the lenses of her glasses. She was looking at him as if he'd dealt her a mortal blow.

Perhaps he shouldn't have told her that he'd been celibate for so long. Certainly, that hadn't helped matters, as she'd appeared genuinely shocked when he'd mentioned it, even upset. He wasn't sure why that was, but no wonder she was shocked. She probably still thought he was the feckless prince he'd once been, indulging himself at every opportunity.

The one who'd begged his brother to swap places with him on the trip his father had insisted they take to the cemetery in the mountains, where all the de Leon kings were buried, in a last-ditch effort to try and instil in Cassius a sense of history and propriety. An understanding of the weight of the name he carried and what it meant, especially after the scandal of his disastrous marriage.

But he'd spent the night before the trip drinking, and had woken up late in the bed of some socialite. He'd called Caspian and bribed him to take his place—a habit they'd got into as boys, as their parents couldn't tell them apart. He had then had gone back to sleep...only to wake a few hours later to the news that the King, Queen and Prince Caspian had been killed in a helicopter crash.

It was his responsibility, no one else's. He might not have caused the crash, but he'd sent his brother to his death all the same, and deprived Aveiras not only of its current king, but of its heir too. There was no coming back from that. There was no fixing it either. All he could do was try his best to make up for what his country had lost.

Inara's pretty mouth opened, and then she shut it again and looked away. He didn't like feeling that he'd hurt her somehow, and it was clear to him that he had.

Of course you have. And telling her she'll simply have to make the best of it isn't helpful.

Perhaps it wasn't. He'd had to deal with his own personal version of hell, because he didn't have another choice. Aveiras had needed a ruler and he had been next in line to the throne. Renouncing the throne at a time of intense public grief would have been unforgivable, so he'd forced down his own personal grief, and the iron weight of his guilt, and he'd done what he had to do. He'd become King, even though it had been the very last thing on earth he'd wanted to do.

Those first few months had been the worst. It hadn't been easy stepping into his brother's shoes, especially considering the public's adoration of Caspian and their low opinion of him, and he hadn't had anyone to help him through it. He'd done it all on his own. But in the end the people had accepted him and, if he hadn't been exactly what they'd wanted, he'd at least managed to get to a point where he wasn't exactly what they *didn't* want.

Still, Inara was young, and if he could spare her having to go through the same fire he had then he would.

'What's upsetting you?' he asked. 'You didn't want a divorce just before and yet now you don't like the idea of staying married. Care to explain?'

She bit her lip, white teeth sinking into all that plush softness, and the simmering desire inside him grew hotter.

He ignored it.

'I just…want things to be the same,' she said hesitantly. 'I don't want to leave the Queen's Estate.'

'I know you don't. But the estate will still be here for you whenever you want to have a holiday.'

'That's not the point. I'm… I'm….' She broke off all of a sudden, her misty grey eyes gone dark and stormy. 'I suppose what I want doesn't matter at all, does it?'

A part of him understood the note of anger in her voice, because he'd felt the same way at having to take the crown. But some things wouldn't be helped by understanding and sympathy. The only way through was acceptance, regardless of one's feelings.

'No,' he said firmly. 'It doesn't. You can't put yourself and what you want before your country, little one.'

She paled even further at that. 'No. That's… that's not what I meant.'

'Then what did you mean? Aveiras needs a queen and, whether you like it or not, that queen is you. Your feelings or otherwise are irrelevant.'

Something passed over her delicate features and then was gone. She looked away, obviously upset.

The tight feeling in his chest constricted further, and he opened his mouth to issue another empty reassurance when she said woodenly, 'I suppose I'll have to pack some clothes, then.'

The urge to touch her cheek or take her hand in comfort gripped him, but he restrained himself. Touching her was a bad idea right now. Perhaps later, when they returned to the palace, he'd take some time to allay any fears she had.

So all he said was, 'Yes, that would be wise. We'll leave for Katara tomorrow morning.'

'So soon?'

'There's no need to wait. The quicker you're installed in the palace, the better.'

Her mouth had a vulnerable look to it, and there was a lost expression on her face, but even as the urge to comfort her intensified her mouth firmed and the lost expression vanished. She drew herself up, small and straight-backed, and when her gaze met his there was nothing misty about it. It was all stone and steel.

'Fine.' Her voice was hard. 'I'll see you in the morning, then.'

Then she turned and went out.

CHAPTER FIVE

INARA DIDN'T SLEEP much that night and woke the next morning with a head full of cotton wool and scratchy eyes. She felt tender between her legs, her inner thigh muscles were sore and there was a certain electricity humming in her blood.

She didn't want to think about Cassius, not when she'd spent most of the night going over and over what had happened between them in the library, but there was no avoiding it this morning.

He'd taken her virginity. He'd decided against a divorce.

He wanted to stay married to her.

She'd be his wife and his queen, not just in name only this time, but for real.

Inara rolled over and tried to burrow her way back underneath the blankets as if she could escape the reality of her situation. But there was no escaping it. What she'd secretly always wanted, had secretly always longed for, was happening, yet in the most nightmarish way possible.

Once again she was being shunted around, at the mercy of other people's decisions, her own thoughts, feelings and opinions not mattering one iota. Her parents had never made any secret of the fact that she was only a tool to them, a disappointment, not the son they'd been counting on, and so it had been her responsibility to make up for it by being useful to them.

It had been bad enough knowing she wasn't what her parents had wanted, but it was a million times worse knowing she wasn't what Cassius wanted. She loved him. She cared about his opinion. And, as he'd pointed out so clearly the night before, she wasn't his choice. He was stuck with her and that hurt.

But of course he wouldn't want a small, stringy, awkward and chaotic maths genius as a queen. He'd want someone tall, beautiful and charming. Someone with perfect manners and all the social graces. Someone with natural authority and dignity, someone who looked the part.

Five years ago when her parents had told her that she was to be promised to Stefano Castelli—after she'd failed to make an impression on the duke's son they'd been eyeing for her— she'd taken matters into her own hands and run away, going straight to the only man in the world she'd thought could help her.

But the man who'd helped her then was the same man who was forcing her into an impossible situation now, and there was nowhere to run to this time.

He was the King. If he wanted to keep her as his wife, as his queen, then he would and there was nothing she could do to stop him.

You'll disappoint him in the end, just as you disappointed your parents. And not just him, but the entire country.

The thought made her feel ill, so she dragged herself out of bed at last and into the shower, hoping that the warm water would help her feel better. But when at last she stepped out, wrapping a towel around her as she wandered back into the bedroom, she still felt as ill as she had when she'd woken up.

The urge to lose herself in the research paper she was currently writing with a colleague in Helsinki gripped her. Numbers were simple. They were clear, logical and had absolutely nothing to do with the confusing mass of emotion currently tangling inside her. But there was no time for that. So she pulled on whatever clothes came to hand, then spent ten minutes packing the rest in a small suitcase.

It wasn't much. After years of having her appearance checked over constantly by her mother, she'd let everything slide while living in the Queen's Estate. It had been a relief not to worry about her hair, or make-up, or her posture, or her dress. Living here meant she was essentially forgotten—which was fine by her. The Queen's Estate was her haven, her refuge.

A cage.

The thought came out of nowhere and for a second was so alien that she looked around to see if someone had spoken it aloud. But, no, apparently that thought had come from her own head, from a deep part of her subconscious even she hadn't known existed.

It was wrong, though. Very, *very* wrong. The Queen's Estate wasn't a cage. How ridiculous. It was her place of safety and she was sad to leave it.

She stuffed a dress into her case, suddenly annoyed. At Cassius and his insistence on his kingly duty. At herself and her decision to seduce him. At the stupid crush she had on him and how that had led her to this moment, forcing her to leave her place of safety for the cold halls of the palace in Katara where her failings would soon become obvious to everyone who looked at her.

Then you have a choice, don't you?

Inara forced the top of the case down and zipped it up, then stood there a second looking down at it.

Cassius had told her the night before that she couldn't put her feelings before her country, and that was very true. It was also very true that she had a choice before her: she could choose to spend her future being miserable and, reluctant and negative about being Queen or, as she couldn't change what would happen, she could choose to accept it. She could choose to try being the kind of queen Cassius wanted. And just because she'd failed her parents, it didn't mean she'd fail him.

After all, hadn't she wanted to be his wife? A real wife, sharing his bed, sharing his life. Having his children, living with him, being with him.

She'd always hoped that being his wife for real would include him being in love with her, but perhaps that would come in time. And if love wasn't on the cards, then she'd settle at least for some respect. That would make being Queen easier, hopefully, and if not it would surely be some consolation?

At that moment there was a knock on her bedroom door that turned out to be Henri, advising her that the helicopter was here to take her to Katara. The King, as it turned out, had left hours earlier to prepare for her arrival, which meant they wouldn't be travelling together.

Inara was relieved. Right now the thought of having to share the tiny space of a helicopter with Cassius was too much for her. She wanted some time alone before she was confronted with him again. Some time to think about how she was going to approach this, because if she decided to accept his decision and take her place as his queen—and really, she had to accept it, because she didn't particularly want to be miserable for the rest of her life—then she needed to figure out how.

Ten minutes later, safely ensconced in the helicopter and flying over the mountains and down towards the coast where the palace was located, Inara decided to put her anxiety about being Queen to one side for now and concentrate instead on being Cassius's actual wife.

And it required some thought, because what did a wife do, exactly?

She only had her own parents' experience to go on, which wasn't encouraging. Their marriage, like their parenting, had been cold, her father interested in nothing but his political machinations, her mother in her social ones. Neither had seemed to like the other much yet they didn't argue. They treated each other with the same chilly politeness with which they treated her.

Would it be like that with Cassius? She knew he wasn't a cold man, or at least he hadn't been the previous night, so maybe it would be different between them.

Except she didn't much like the gentle condescension he'd been affecting with her the past couple of years. Perhaps once they started living together as husband and wife that might change.

Although…would they be living together as husband and wife? All Cassius had said was that she would remain his wife and take her place as queen. Did that involve living together? Sharing a bed? Or would they have separate rooms at the palace? Would they only meet for formal occasions and official functions, continuing on with their separate lives? Or would they spend time together outside of those times? Alone with each other. The way they used to…

Longing curled in Inara's heart.

Yes, that was what she wanted. A marriage like that—talking together, easy and friendly. Laughing and discussing things of interest, with the occasional argument that didn't get too serious. Not her parents' icy formality, but something warmer and more real. Friendlier.

And sex. You want that too.

Inara shifted on the seat cushions, remembering the night before—Cassius beneath her, all long, lean muscle and power, looking at her with fire in his eyes. Looking at her the way she'd desperately wanted him to for so long. Him moving inside her, giving her the most intense pleasure…

Heat prickled over her skin. Yes, okay, maybe she wanted that as well. But…would he? Would a marriage to him include that? Or was what they'd shared together in the library a one-off thing that wouldn't happen again?

He'd said that he hadn't had a lover in three years, that she was the first one he'd taken in all that time, so surely...? But then again, if he'd managed to go without sex for so long then perhaps he didn't need it...

No, there were too many variables, that was the problem, and too much she didn't know. The answers to those questions could only be solved by more research, and that meant talking to him, which she would have to do when they landed.

Feeling somewhat better now that she'd thought a few things through, Inara watched as they flew over Katara, the capital city of Aveiras.

It was famously beautiful, with a historic walled town located near the central business district and by the sea. The old palace was the centrepiece of the old town, built out of weathered white stone with beautifully laid-out formal gardens. It was the seat of the royal family of Aveiras and had been for centuries. Inara had always disliked it.

Despite how picturesque it looked, the palace had felt cold and echoing and unfriendly whenever she'd visited and, as the helicopter descended to the helipad located in the palace grounds, creeping doubt wound through her.

Regardless of what kind of wife she would be, she would also be Queen. What would the palace staff think of the King's decision? What would the people of Aveiras think? Cassius's mother had been revered and deeply loved, and her death had been bitterly mourned. No one would want Inara stepping into her shoes, surely?

A phalanx of palace staff waited as the helicopter landed, and as soon as she stepped out they surrounded her, taking her one pathetic suitcase and shepherding her towards the doors that led into the palace. All of them looked business-like and not one smiled at her. It made her homesick for the Queen's Estate, where there was no one to look at her and judge her. No one to disappoint. Only Henri and Joan, who cared about her.

And now you have no one...

The thought threw dark shadows everywhere so she pushed it away, hoping that Cassius might come to meet her. But it was soon clear that he wouldn't, so she told herself it was fine and she didn't mind. He was the King. He probably had better things to do, and anyway, though it would have been nice to see a friendly face in amongst the crowd of grim-looking palace employees, she didn't need it. She would manage. Of course she would. She would have to.

Inara was ushered down the long, echoing stone hallways of the palace with high-vaulted ceilings and long lines of dark, formal portraits of the de Leon royal line. The chill of the palace crept into her bones as she walked, though she tried not to let it, and the disapproving gazes of the people in the portraits followed her.

The palace had always felt oppressive, and it wasn't any different now, the heavy weight of history and its judgment pressing down on her. It reminded her of being in her parents' house and the constant critical attention they had subjected her to—always measuring her, always judging her.

And this is now your home.

Inara did her best not to think of that.

Eventually she was led to the royal apartments and ushered into what turned out to be a rather pleasant sitting room located in a part of the large, sprawling palace that overlooked the famous Aveiran white cliffs and the deep blue of the sea that lay below them.

Inara had never visited the royal apartments

and had always assumed they would be just as cold and empty and echoing as the rest of the palace. But this room was neither cold nor empty nor echoing.

It had large windows that looked out over a small but beautiful and slightly overgrown garden full of flowers, with the jewel-blue sea beyond it. There were rugs on the floor that echoed the colour of the flowers outside, and a couple of deep, comfortable-looking chairs upholstered in dark-blue velvet, with a matching sofa. Cushions had been scattered artfully everywhere and bookcases full of books stood against the bare stone walls. And most surprising of all, on the side tables, sideboard and numerous shelves, there was a plethora of small shrubs in decorative pots. The plants softened the atmosphere, making it seem lived-in and inviting, even though the whole room reeked of a tidiness that was foreign to Inara.

She took a few steps over to the windows and glanced out at the early afternoon steadily advancing.

Nerves coiled tightly inside her. Presumably she'd been brought here to…what? Wait? For whom—Cassius? Or would someone else come for her? And what was she supposed to do, exactly?

Inara swallowed, her hands closing into fists. She hated not knowing things and there was nothing worse than questions she didn't know the answers to. Especially when the answers were dependent on someone else who wasn't around. It meant there was nothing to stop her brain from throwing up yet more questions until her thought processes were going round and round like mice running on a wheel.

It didn't help that, along with her nerves, there was also a strange, prickling sense of anticipation, the same feeling she got whenever she knew Cassius was coming to visit, except not quite.

Before, she'd been full of a simple joy. Now, the joy was tempered with other things, more complicated things. Nerves and a little rush of fear, along with heat and a strange sort of excitement. Normally when she felt this way she retreated into her research, but she couldn't do that now, so to relieve the tension Inara walked slowly over to one of the tables to examine a tiny, gnarled bonsai in a blue glazed pot that sat on it.

Too busy looking at the bonsai, she didn't hear the door click softly behind her.

'Inara,' Cassius's deep, authoritative voice said from behind her. 'Welcome to the palace.'

She hadn't dressed for the occasion, Cassius observed with some disapproval as Inara straightened from looking at the bonsai juniper that sat on the table near the couch.

She looked as if she'd pulled on any old thing that had come to hand, which in this instance was a pair of worn jeans and pale pink T-shirt with a coffee stain on the front of it. Her silvery hair was caught in a simple ponytail at the nape of her neck and she wore no make-up whatsoever.

Yet still desire gripped him by the throat, refusing to let go as a deeply possessive, very male part of him noted how closely the T-shirt moulded to her figure, highlighting the soft roundness of her breasts and the elegant curve of her waist. The jeans, though they were entirely unsuitable for a queen, certainly made him want to put a hand on her pretty rear and squeeze her gently.

Unacceptable.

He hadn't slept much the night before, having left the Queen's Estate at dawn so he could get back to the palace as quickly as possible in order to prepare for Inara's arrival. Also, if he was honest with himself, to get rid of the heat that lingered in his blood whenever he thought of her.

He'd thought having the entire morning to prepare and then attend to his other duties would have dealt with any remaining lustful thoughts, but apparently that had just been a convenient lie he'd told himself.

Apparently all that was needed for those thoughts to roar back into life was her physical presence, in simple jeans and a T-shirt no less.

It was unseemly. He needed to control himself, to discourage his baser instincts, not look at her hungrily, thinking about what he'd like to do to her. He should remember that he was the leader of a nation and not a teenage boy with more hormones than sense.

It was a good thing he'd spent some time this morning deciding on an appropriate code of conduct between them, which was why he'd brought her here, to one of his favourite rooms in the palace. He hoped she'd find it a relaxing environment in which to be informed of her duties as Queen and what the shape of her future at the palace would look like. Also his expectations of her as his wife, a subject he'd given much thought.

Since returning from the Queen's Estate, he'd immediately informed his council and parliament of his intention to remain married and for Inara to stay on as Aveiras's queen. This had prompted some disapproval, which he'd expected, and he'd had to put his foot down about the decision. However, he was hoping that a strict regimen of stylists and lessons in protocol and etiquette would soon sand the sharp edges off and make Inara more palatable to both his parliament and his people.

It was important to him that they accept her, especially when they'd already had to accept him, the black sheep of his illustrious family. He'd been hoping to give them a queen they could love, like they'd loved his mother, but as that was now out of the question he hoped to give them a queen that they could tolerate at the very least.

Being patient was key. Inara needed some time to come to terms with her new position and to learn her official duties, and that couldn't be rushed. In the meantime, he'd organised a small function to present her to his court and his parliament. Nothing too formal or too large, but enough to remind people that Inara was their queen and would remain so.

Already, gossip about her was rife, and he'd decided that wasn't a bad thing. The more people talked about her, the more she'd be in the public consciousness. She'd be a novelty at first, but then she'd become ubiquitous, as he had.

She turned from the bonsai, her eyes wide behind the lenses of her glasses. Then she straightened and her shoulders went back, as if bracing herself. 'Hello, Cassius,' she said, her sweet voice very formal.

He frowned. Something was missing. And it took him a moment or two to realise that what was missing was the smile she always gave him whenever she saw him—the warm, joyful one. The one that made him feel as if he was a bright spot in her particular world. The one that made him feel like a friend. Like a person instead of a figurehead.

Why would you want to be a person? Es-

pecially the person who caused his brother's death...

Cassius shoved that thought away.

'The palace staff will bring us a late lunch shortly,' he said. 'I thought it might be easier for you to have an informal meal for your first day in the palace. It will also give us some time to discuss what happens now.'

'Oh. Uh...yes, that would be very...pleasant.' She shifted on her feet, a pink flush staining her cheeks. 'I don't know where my suitcase is.'

The suitcase in question had been taken to the Queen's apartments, though if she'd only brought one case then there hadn't been much point in bringing anything. Not when he'd provide her with everything she needed.

'It's in the Queen's rooms,' he said. 'Which will be exclusively for your use, of course. At night, however, you will share mine.'

She blinked rapidly. 'Yours?'

'Yes. Not right away, of course,' he allowed. 'You will need some time to feel comfortable with me, and I understand that. But you will be my wife, Inara. And that does not mean separate beds.'

It was something he'd thought long and hard

about, especially after his lapse in the library with her. Grief and shock had killed his desire, and three years of abstinence hadn't helped. But now it had returned and with such a vengeance that it was clear he needed an outlet for it. He needed someone in his bed and, logically, that someone should be his wife.

It was convenient that she was the one he wanted, too. Perhaps if he had her in his bed every night he'd be better able to control himself, not let himself become so desperate that he'd fall back into old habits.

'Oh,' she said again. 'I suppose so.'

It shouldn't have been a source of irritation that she didn't look entirely happy with the suggestion, but he was irritated all the same. It was an emotion he had no right to, of course. He'd been the one to take her innocence the night before, to lose control. He'd thought of no one but himself and his own pleasure and, if he needed yet another lesson in what a mistake that was, he was looking at it right now.

It's no less than what you deserve.

Oh, he was well aware. Being King was his penance and one he undertook willingly.

Cassius ignored his irritation. 'If you're not

comfortable with that tonight, you may sleep in the Queen's rooms,' he said levelly. 'But I should warn you that this will not be a union of convenience only, not now.'

'I see. Well, I understand. And no need for me to go to the Queen's rooms tonight.' Something hot gleamed in her eyes, a little spark.

So it seemed she was happy being in his bed after all.

Careful.

Yes, he needed the reminder, because already the smouldering embers of his desire were beginning to ignite in response to that spark. It wouldn't take much for them to burst into flame…a kiss, a touch…

The thread of unease he'd felt when he'd walked in wound tighter.

His desire for her was more…consuming than he'd expected it to be and he didn't like that one bit. This wasn't the library at the Queen's Estate. This was the palace, where he was king, and a king shouldn't be so desperate to sleep with his wife that he literally couldn't think of anything else.

That was the man talking and the man couldn't be trusted. He knew that already.

Perhaps he shouldn't have her in his bed to-night after all. Perhaps he should use tonight to remind the man of how a king should act so that, when she finally joined him, it would be the king who'd be in control.

Besides, she could probably use a night to ad-just to her new position too, no matter that little spark in her eyes.

He strolled over to the windows, paused to glance out at the blue sea, then carried on over to the fireplace, Inara watching him all the while.

It made him uncomfortable. Made him feel oddly transparent, as if she could see the exact nature of his restlessness. As if she knew that the title of king was just a mask he wore, and a badly fitting mask at that. As if she could see beneath that mask to the same careless prince he'd once been. A man driven by his own self-ish desires and desperately unsuited to be the ruler he now was. A man who hadn't respected the throne or the role he'd been given to play.

A man whose own brother was dead because of him.

It was a good thing *that* man was now as dead as Caspian.

Cassius met her gaze, his mask firmly in place.

'Good. I have drawn up a schedule for you this week, which will involve a stylist and wardrobe consultation, meetings with the palace PR people, media training plus protocol and etiquette instruction. That won't be enough time to prepare you for a formal royal ball, but it should allow you to feel more comfortable at the small gathering I've organised to reintroduce you to my court.'

A flicker of unhappy surprise crossed her face. 'A…small gathering? How small?'

'It's nothing,' he said dismissively. 'A couple of hundred people. Not many.'

'A couple of hundred…' She looked abruptly down at the floor. 'No,' she said as if to herself. 'No, I can do that.'

Cassius, expecting an argument, was thrown off balance. 'I know it's not what you particularly enjoy but—'

'It's part of being a queen,' she interrupted, brisker this time. 'I understand.' She lifted her gaze back to his, somehow standing even straighter. 'I'll do it. I can manage. And I… I'm sorry about my behaviour yesterday in the library. When you suggested I take on royal duties, I was…shocked. And a bit scared. I've been

living at the Queen's Estate for five years and…
well…change is always difficult. But, as you
said, neither of us has a choice about this, so
I'm going to try.' Her chin lifted. 'I want to be
a good queen for Aveiras and I'm going to work
hard not to let you down.'

Surprise rippled through him. He'd expected
her to give in at some point, because he wouldn't
be moved on this, but he'd thought he'd have to
insist or perhaps argue with her.

He studied her, aware of something shifting
inside him. A curiosity he hadn't been conscious
of before. She'd always been an open book to
him, but this was…different. 'What brought this
on? You weren't at all happy about it yesterday.'

'I know.' She shoved her hands into the back
pockets of her jeans, her feet moving about as if
she couldn't figure out how to stand. His mother
would have found that appalling. She had been a
stickler for correct behaviour, and fidgeting was
not correct behaviour, especially not for a queen.

'I've had some time to think about it,' Inara
went on, oblivious to her bad posture. 'And
you were right about having to accept things.
About putting my feelings before my country,

too. Aveiras needs a queen, and I'm that queen whether I like it or not.'

Cassius knew he should have been happy that she'd made peace with his decision, that she was willing to try being the queen Aveiras needed. Yet her little speech irritated him. Had he been expecting something more, something he could fight her on? Did he *want* to fight her?

Ridiculous. He didn't want a fight. The last few years his parents had been alive had been a constant battle against his father's repeated calls for him to display some kind of restraint—especially after his 'ill-conceived marriage', as his father had termed it. He'd accused Cassius of disrespecting the crown, accused him of loving himself more than he loved his country.

His father hadn't been wrong. Cassius had taken great pleasure in disobeying his father's rules and strictures, even making a game out of it with mocking statements, snide observations, sarcastic sound bites and compromising press photos. And the worst part about it was that now he barely even remembered why he'd done all those things.

One thing he was sure of was that he didn't do them any longer, and neither did he fight.

He didn't lose himself to anger—or indeed any emotion inappropriate to his position—so he shouldn't be regretting his wife's capitulation, not at all. He wanted this to go smoothly and easily, and the fewer challenges from her the better.

Yet, despite what he wanted, he still felt restless and irritable, moving from the fireplace and pacing over to one of the tables where he kept another bonsai, a cherry blossom. Reflexively, he looked the miniature tree over, taking note of the soil conditions and the tree itself. Tending plants was useful for all kinds of emotional disturbances. Sometimes he preferred more physical outlets, such as swimming endless laps of the palace pool, or running for miles on the treadmill in the gym, but when that was impossible he liked to come into this room and check over the pots. It focused his mind and helped him concentrate. Helped him stay in control.

He'd done that even as a boy, when the interminable school-room lessons that Caspian had seemed to handle with no problem had become too much for him. He'd never been able to sit still and concentrate for long before the need to move would take him, so he'd disappear into the gardens, hiding out with the head gardener, who used to take him on a tour of all the plants.

It had calmed him then and it calmed him now.

He picked up a tiny pair of scissors and trimmed part of the tree carefully.

Inara wandered over and watched him. 'What are you doing?'

He snipped off a tiny branch. 'Trimming the bonsai so it retains its shape.'

'Oh. Do you do that yourself then?'

'Yes.'

She peered at the tree. 'Why? Don't you have staff to do everything for you?'

He'd never had to explain his interest in plants to anyone. No one had ever asked. Not many people—apart from the staff who tended to the King's private rooms—even knew about his hobby. He didn't like to talk about it, not when it revealed certain things about him, and still less to someone as sharp and intelligent as Inara.

Still, not answering was also revealing, so he said, trying not to sound reluctant, 'I make a lot of decisions that impact a lot of people and I have to do that every day. Tending to a few plants that don't require much beyond watering and some nutrients is a nice change.'

'I see.' She glanced around at the pots scattered everywhere. 'Are all these yours?'

'Yes.' She was standing quite close and he caught a faint hint of delicate musk in the air, along with the flowery scent of her shampoo. It sent a thread of heat through him.

'Wow. They look amazing.'

She sounded genuine, and when he glanced at her the expression on her face made it clear that her admiration was, in fact, genuine. And he was shocked by the warmth that bloomed abruptly behind his breastbone, as if part of him enjoyed her praise. As if he almost…needed it.

And why not, when you never had any as a boy? Only relentless, constant criticism.

That was true. He hadn't had much praise in his life, not as a boy and not as a man. He'd more often been told of the many ways he didn't measure up, never about the things he did that were right, and in the end he'd stopped caring. What was the point in trying to measure up to a standard you'd never achieve? Or constantly trying to be something you weren't? Better to embrace who you actually were instead. Accept yourself, as no one else would.

He'd told himself he didn't need to be praised,

that he didn't care what anyone thought of him, and he believed that. So he had no idea why this one woman's obvious delight in his house plants should please him so much. It was ridiculous.

No, you know why. Her opinion has always been important. Right from the very first moment she climbed into your limo and looked at you like you were her own personal saviour.

'It's just water and the right fertiliser,' he said dismissively, ignoring the voice in his head.

'No, it's not.' Inara shook her head, staring down at the cherry blossom he'd been pruning. 'If it was that simple, all my plants wouldn't die. I have a black thumb.' Gently she reached out and touched one of the blossoms on the tree. 'Numbers I can figure out. But taking care of a plant, not so much.'

'Numbers are slightly more important than keeping a few house plants alive.'

She lifted a shoulder. 'I guess. Sometimes. But they're not exactly practical, are they?'

He remembered suddenly a similar discussion they'd had years ago, about her university studies. She'd been having a small crisis of confidence about her master's thesis and he'd tried to encourage her, even though he'd had no idea how he, a man who was more interested in parties and women, could possibly make her feel better about her own phenomenal intellectual abilities.

He'd made a joke out of it, made her laugh, though he'd known even back then it was simply to cover up his own inadequacies.

Now, he didn't feel so inadequate, yet it was clear she still had the same doubts. Where had those come from?

Ah, but he knew. Her family. They'd been so obsequious when he'd married her, both parents bowing and scraping, and making much of the fact that they'd never expected their daughter to do so well for herself as to marry a prince. They hadn't cared that he was over ten years her senior. They hadn't seemed to care much about their fiercely intelligent daughter at all, or know what to do with her beyond marrying her off for social gain.

You didn't really know what to do with her either.

He did now. He was going to turn her into his queen.

'I'm sure we can find some practical applications,' he said. 'And in the meantime, with a bit of polish and some deportment lessons, you'll do a very fine and practical job of being a queen.'

Inara glanced up at him, her expression solemn. 'I'm going to try, Cassius. I promise.'

He could feel the warmth of her body. See the pulse beating at the base of her pale throat. She stood so close to him that the curve of her breast nearly pressed against his arm.

Heat licked through him, and just like that his control was hanging by a thread. And he knew that all the concentration in the world on his damn plants wasn't going to make a difference. That he wanted her right here, right now. On the floor before the empty fireplace. Her clothes ripped away, those delicate limbs wrapped around him, her body welcoming his, clutching him tightly as he drove himself inside her. Giving him pleasure for just a little while...

But no. That was the man talking. The flawed, selfish man, motivated by his own crude appetites and base emotions. He couldn't allow the man to gain control again.

A king was above that. A king was better than that. He had to be. And so must Cassius.

He put down the scissors carefully and straightened. 'I think tonight I'll allow you some time to get comfortable in the Queen's private apartments.' His voice was cold, but he couldn't help that. 'If you need anything, please don't hesitate to let the palace staff know.'

Then he strode from the room before the thread on his control snapped completely.

CHAPTER SIX

INARA DID NOT enjoy the following week. The lessons in protocol and etiquette were boring and, no matter how hard she tried, she couldn't remember the names and lineages of all the people she'd be introduced to, still less their potted family histories.

She kept curtseying when she shouldn't curtsey at all, or bowing when she should have extended a hand. She walked too fast, walked too slowly, laughed when she shouldn't and so on.

It was all far too similar to the lessons her mother had drilled into her, complaining that, for a mathematical genius, she was very stupid. How could she remember formulae when she couldn't remember one person's name?

Inara hadn't known the answer then and she didn't now. All she could do was try, but it felt as if her brain was made of Swiss cheese and all the important things kept leaking out through the holes.

The meetings with the PR people were as bad—lots of advice on what to say and what to do, most of which she couldn't remember. She'd hoped the time she'd spend with the stylist would be better, but no. Her opinion on different outfits was needed, plus she had to keep still as she was measured and pinned to within an inch of her life.

She had no time to herself. No time for her research, to rest her brain in the cold, clean air of numbers where she could lose herself.

It was awful and she hated it.

Of course, it would also have been a million times more bearable if she could have spoken to Cassius—however briefly—but he was absent the entire week.

He seemed to have retreated from her like a mirage, vanishing into offices and receiving rooms, constantly surrounded by advisors and courtiers. Forever meeting dignitaries and heads of state. Always in some kind of meeting or other.

She barely caught a glimpse of him.

She'd tried asking one of his aides if she could speak with him, but was told his schedule was full for the week, and that he would see her the night of her official presentation.

Inara couldn't shake the sense that he was avoiding her. The night she'd arrived he'd been very clear about what he wanted, going on about lessons and etiquette, and something about a formal presentation. But the only thing that had caught her full attention was that he expected them to share a bed.

She'd wanted that too, very much, and then quite suddenly, just as they were having a perfectly lovely conversation, he'd changed his mind. Without explanation. A staff member had come in within seconds of Cassius's departure, ushering her through to the Queen's private apartments and leaving her there.

Inara hadn't minded that night. Instead she'd explored her new home, confident that the next day he'd come and find her and then perhaps they'd start their married life together.

But he hadn't. It had been an aide instead, armed with a schedule, who'd chivvied her from one lesson to another, pleading ignorance whenever she attempted to ask about Cassius.

And he hadn't come that night either. Or the one after that. Or the one after that. And, as the days had gone by, she'd gradually realised that he wasn't going to come for her at all.

Inara ignored her disappointment, told herself he'd come for her when he was ready and, in the meantime, she'd do her best to be what he wanted. But as time had gone on and no word had come, she'd become less and less sure that he'd ever send for her. Less and less sure that he'd ever wanted her.

Less and less sure that he wanted a wife at all.

Perhaps he didn't. He'd said that it wouldn't be a union of convenience, and yet nearly a week later she was still on her own. Still in the Queen's apartments, with its delicate, spindly furniture and hard floors of polished marble. With its echoing, vaulted spaces and views over the regimented lines of the formal gardens.

Still alone.

He'd forgotten about her. The way he always did.

Inara didn't want that to ache like a thorn in her heart. But it did. He'd made such a big deal out of their marriage, about her coming to Katara to live at the palace, about her being Queen, and she'd accepted it. She'd put aside her own wishes, swallowed her fear, held on to her courage and left her home of nearly five years to come to the palace she hated.

And he'd ignored her almost completely.

She knew she had no claim on him, that their marriage had never been one of the heart, yet she'd thought he was her friend at least. Certainly after that night in the library, when he'd taken her virginity, she'd expected there to be… some kind of bond. That he'd at least think of her at some point.

But, no. Apparently not.

If she'd needed further proof that he felt nothing for her, then his silence and his absence confirmed it. She even started to doubt she'd see him the night of her first appearance as Queen.

Sure enough, when the night itself arrived, she was scrubbed and plucked and made up, then zipped into her gown without any mention of him. Then she was ushered down more long, echoing palace hallways and into a small, cold room off the main ballroom, where her aide told her to wait before disappearing, leaving Inara none the wiser as to why she had to wait here or what was going to happen next.

The room was empty of anything save some gloomy formal paintings and an icy-looking marble fireplace covered in too much gilt. Through the closed double doors that led to the ballroom, she could hear people laughing and talking and the delicate sounds of music.

It made her feel sick, made everything she'd been taught during the whole vile week go straight out of her head—not that it had ever been in her head to start with. Her palms were sweaty and she felt as though she were encased in armour instead of a glittering confection of a gown, all silvery tulle with silver embroidery and crystals sewn into the frothy skirts. Her hair had been piled on top of her head, a delicate diamond tiara set among her curls, and she didn't want to move too quickly or tip her head in case the whole thing came tumbling down. The pins hurt and her eyes felt dry and sore with the new contact lenses.

She felt like a little girl dressing up in her mother's clothes, the way she always had back when she'd been trotted out to all the parties her mother had insisted she attend.

Her mother had said that everything—even her—could be improved with a pretty dress, yet for some reason there had never been a dress that could magically improve Inara, and it was likely this dress wouldn't either.

What would they all think when she walked into the ballroom? What would they be expecting? Probably the child bride their prince had married so foolishly all those years ago and had since forgotten.

Inara had begun to tremble with nerves when the door that led to the corridor opened and Cassius walked in. He was, as usual, surrounded by people, but he lifted a hand and they all withdrew, leaving her alone with him at last.

It had been a full week since she'd seen him in that lovely room with all the plants, and the impact of his presence was almost a physical force.

He was dressed formally, in tailored black evening clothes with no adornments bar the royal crest of the de Leon family—a set of scales signifying justice set in a jewelled pin on his lapel.

The ascetic lines of his clothing only emphasised the sheer masculine beauty of the man who wore them—his height, the width and breadth of his shoulders and chest, the lean span of his waist and the powerful length of his long legs.

His charisma was a palpable thing, regal, commanding and utterly authoritative. It made Inara's knees weak, and her heart beat far too fast. And, when his smoky amber gaze met hers, something inside her burst into flame.

She forgot her nerves. Forgot the ball in her honour happening just outside the doors. Forgot the entire week of hell she'd endured and how he'd ignored her. She forgot everything except that at last they were in the same room.

'C-Cassius,' she stuttered, taking a helpless step towards him. 'You're here.'

'Of course.' His deep voice was as cool and measured as ever, the perfect lines of his face revealing nothing but calm. 'Where else would I be?'

He was the only familiar thing she'd seen all week, and she wanted very badly to get close to him, to put a hand on his broad, hard chest and take some of his strength, some of his control and authority, for herself.

Except there was something about him that held her rooted to the spot, an icy distance that made her certain he wouldn't like her touching him one bit.

Inara swallowed, closing her hands into fists to stop herself from wiping them on her glittering gown. 'I…wasn't sure. I've been trying to see you all week, but everyone kept saying you were busy.'

'I was busy. Didn't they tell you that I'd see you tonight?'

'Yes, but—'

'But what?' One imperious black brow rose.

'But...' She stopped.

He looked so unapproachable, so untouchable. Would he really want to hear about how homesick she felt, about and how nervous she'd been and still was? How hard she'd found this week, trying to remember all the things she had to do and say and in what order?

A few years ago she wouldn't have thought twice about confiding in him. Maybe even a few months ago. But now...it felt different. They were in the palace, in his territory, and he was the King. The heavy gold ring of state was on his right hand, and he was looking at her as if she was merely a poor petitioner come before his throne rather than his queen...

'Nothing,' she said at last, her mouth dry. 'It's fine.'

Cassius surveyed her for a second, his gaze inscrutable as it drifted from her elaborately curled hair and tiara, down over the strapless, embroidered silver bodice of her gown to the layers of tulle and crystal of its skirts.

She had no idea what he thought of it, or whether he approved, but she wanted him to be impressed with her. To think she looked like a queen at least. To think that she was beautiful…

Are you crazy? Why would he ever think that, when even your own mother thought you were at best only acceptable?

She shoved the thought out of her head, trying to force down how intimidated she felt in his presence and how the apprehension about the moment they would step out into the ballroom was getting to her. How ill it was making her.

She'd do this because that was what she'd promised him. To be his queen, one who hopefully would shame neither him nor Aveiras. Because this was important to him and she didn't want to disappoint him.

Not like she'd disappointed everyone else.

So she didn't speak about any of her fears, trying not to let his lack of reaction get to her. When he presented his arm, she took it, resisting clutching at it like an over-anxious child. Then they turned towards the double doors, which were then thrown open, the glittering lights and noise of the ball crashing over her like a wave.

'His Royal Majesty, King Cassius,' the usher announced loudly as the noise of the crowd quietened. 'And Her Royal Majesty, Queen Inara.'

And, whether she wanted to or not, Inara found herself being drawn relentlessly into the ballroom.

Inara was so bright he couldn't even look at her. He didn't dare. She was small and delicate and exquisite in a silver confection of a gown that looked as though it had been scattered with stardust. And she, alabaster-pale, her grey eyes luminous, was the star.

He'd thought a week of avoiding her would put some distance between him and his unnervingly powerful desire, but it hadn't. The moment he'd stepped into that room and set eyes on her, watched the bright, joyful thing ignite in her eyes when he looked at her, everything possessive, hungry and desperate had roared up inside him and demanded its due.

It should have been enough, burying himself in all those impossible, endless meetings that he loathed with a passion, the never-ending round of requests made, answers he must give, decisions he must make. The constant procession of audiences and petitions and grievances and complaints...

All those duties, the duties of a king, should have reminded him how petty were his own passions and appetites. How unimportant next to the needs of his country. Yet all he'd been able to think about was how he wanted to cancel every meeting he had to go looking for her. To go hunting for her, to catch her and drag her from the Queen's apartments and into his bed.

But he knew himself too well and how those base desires and primitive emotions could take hold. They were all-consuming. They'd once made him put the pursuit of them before his family, before his country. They were flaws.

And a king had to be flawless.

So he tried to ignore the woman on his arm, so bright and glittering, delicate and beautiful, as he guided her around the ballroom and introduced her to the important people of his court. And, because he couldn't look at her, he didn't see how pale she'd become under the glittering crystals of the chandelier, or notice how she kept looking at him whenever he spoke someone's name. He told himself that he didn't need to pay attention, because all those etiquette and protocol lessons and PR consultations would have given her everything she needed to handle this little soiree.

Nerves were expected, so he didn't worry when she stammered, curtseyed to someone instead of shaking their hand or looked bewildered when she called the Prime Minister by someone else's name, then appeared to forget that Aveiras even had a prime minister.

As the evening wore on, he could hear people whispering, and caught the looks of disapproval sent their way as Inara forgot yet another name, and then used the wrong title, and then stopped speaking altogether.

He told himself that it would get better for her, that this was a rite of passage she had to bear and that, once it was done, she'd find things easier, but for some reason all those things sounded like hollow justifications.

It never got easier for you.

No, but he'd been thrown in at the deep end after the accident and, faced with drowning, he'd simply learned how to swim. Inara wasn't in the deep end and she'd had a whole week's preparation. And she had him at her side. It wasn't the same at all.

Except it was becoming apparent that, despite what he'd told himself, Inara was a long way from learning to swim in these particular waters.

After she made yet another mistake with a name, he finally forced himself to look at her. She was so pale and her eyes looked red and irritated. Her shoulders were tense and she held herself awkwardly, her movements stiff and unsure.

She seemed to jolt suddenly as his gaze rested on her, as if she'd just become aware of his attention, making a sharp, involuntary movement that looked almost like a flinch, and knocking some woman's elbow and the wine glass she was holding out of her hand. The glass smashed on the marble floor, red wine splashing everywhere like blood.

The music stopped, people pausing in their conversations to look in Inara's direction.

A terrible, awful silence fell.

She stood there in her beautiful gown, red wine staining her skirts, an expression of utter horror on her face. 'I—I'm so sorry,' she stammered, white as a sheet and trembling.

Cassius put out a hand to her, but she ignored him, turning without a word and running straight through the massive double doors that led to the terrace and the formal gardens beyond.

Whispers began, the wind of disapproval blowing through the ballroom, heads turning, attention focusing. Everyone looked at him and he knew they'd be gauging his response, wondering how he'd handle this unseemly display.

This is your fault. You ignored her all week, because you couldn't handle yourself in her presence, and now look what's happened. She wasn't ready and you threw her to the wolves.

Yes, he'd done that. This mess *was* his fault. He'd ignored her because he didn't like the way she'd made him want her, leaving her in the hands of palace employees who clearly hadn't done a good enough job of preparing her. He should have overseen her lessons or at least checked in on her.

Well, if the court wanted to see his response to the Queen's chaotic and abrupt departure, then he would show them.

Allowing no emotion to be displayed on his face, Cassius murmured to the aide at his elbow, then proceeded to soothe the ruffled feathers of the woman whose arm had been knocked. Palace employees rushed in to sweep up the glass, and within moments the music had resumed, conversation buzzed again and the ball went on as if nothing had happened.

Five minutes later, once attention on him had shifted, Cassius told his aide curtly that he'd be seeing to the Queen, before striding from the ballroom after her. The ball could go on without him for a while, especially as the whole reason for the ball in the first place had disappeared.

Outside, even though it was night, the discreet lighting of the formal gardens ensured that it wasn't completely dark. Fountains played, and beneath their delicate music he could hear the sound of the sea crashing against the white cliffs below the palace.

He couldn't see Inara anywhere, though he searched all the places in the gardens where she might have gone, the stone benches near the fountains and beside the rose beds. The pretty archway of bougainvillea. The magnolia copse.

At last he came to a pavilion of white stone

that stood on the cliffs, looking out over the ocean. He gave it a cursory glance, because it didn't look as if anyone was inside, then stopped, his gaze caught by a slight glitter.

In the shadow of one of the pillars, sitting on the stone bench with her skirts caught around her, was Inara. Her head was turned away, her gaze on the ocean throwing itself against the cliffs.

Despite it being late summer, the sea breeze was cool, so he moved over to where she sat, shrugging out of his jacket as he went so he could drape it around her pale shoulders.

She turned her head as he approached, obviously hearing his step. Even though she hurriedly wiped her face, he could see the tears there.

You hurt her. Like you hurt everyone close to you.

His heart twisted hard with a familiar pain. Well, that was nothing new, but at least with Inara he could do something about it.

He came closer, holding his jacket out, but she shook her head, her tiara slipping to one side. 'No. Stay where you are.' Her voice sounded thick. 'Just…give me five minutes.'

Cassius stopped. 'Inara.'

'I'll come back, I promise.' She surreptitiously wiped at her face. 'I hope that lady was okay. I didn't mean to knock her elbow, I just... I don't know what happened.'

'Inara,' he said again.

'I'm sorry. I tried, I really did, but when I told you I wasn't good in social situations, well, I meant it.'

He stood there stiffly, holding his jacket in one hand, staring at her small figure curled up on the stone bench. Remembering her white face and her red eyes. The feel of her fingers on his arm, clutching at him.

Remembering joining her in that little room before the ball, reeling from the gut punch of her beauty and trying not to show it. Trying not to see the way she looked at him, as if for reassurance. Trying not to hear the hurt in her voice as she told him that she'd asked for him...

She's always looked at you as if you were her hero. And you let her down.

His stomach dropped away, the truth of it settling in his heart. Denying the man had worked very well for three years. He'd controlled his appetites, excised the selfishness from his heart and, following his brother's example, he'd done everything he could to become a perfect king. But that didn't allow for much else. It certainly didn't allow for a woman who was new to royal duties, who hadn't been brought up with them the way he had.

A woman who was only here because of him and the mistake he'd made. He couldn't fix what had happened with Caspian, but he could fix what happened with Inara. He'd lost control with her when he shouldn't have and, while nothing could change that fact, he could admit that the decision to keep her at arm's length had clearly been a foolish one.

He'd decided she would be his queen, but Inara wasn't a princess brought up in the palace spotlight. She was a girl he'd married at sixteen and left to her own devices in an isolated manor house in the countryside for the best part of five years. Throwing her into court on her own after a mere week's training, and expecting her to behave like a woman born to it, was ludicrous.

Worse, it was selfish, because it was about his own discomfort rather than anything to do with her. And it had hurt her. His control was usually excellent these days. Yes, he'd lost it with her once, but that didn't mean he'd lose it every single time. And, anyway, he wanted heirs. How could he get those heirs if he avoided taking her to his bed?

She was his wife. His bed was where she belonged and it was high time he showed her that. Without a word, Cassius strode over to her and draped his jacket around her shoulders.

She looked up, her eyes wide. 'What are you doing? Just give me another minute and I'll come—'

'You're not going anywhere except back to my rooms,' he said coolly. Then he bent and picked her up in his arms.

Inara stiffened, twisting in his grip. 'Put me down. I don't want…'

'Hush.' He tightened his hold, keeping her safe against his chest. 'We won't be returning to the ball. We're going to my apartments where we can talk in peace.'

She took a breath and he could feel the resistance bleed out of her, her small, delicate frame going limp against him. 'I'll get wine on your clothes.'

'I don't care.'

He stepped out of the pavilion, making his

way through the dimly lit gardens, conscious of how warm she was, and how beneath the acrid smell of spilled red wine he detected the faint musky scent that was Inara.

It made him feel hungry and possessive, like a leopard with its kill. Ordinarily he would have ignored that kind of feeling. He would have pushed it away. But not tonight.

Avoiding the ballroom, Cassius entered the palace through a side door. He nodded to the guards stationed on either side and strode on down the corridors, heading towards his private apartments.

'I'm sorry,' Inara said, a bitter note in her voice. 'I failed.'

He glanced down. Her head rested against his shoulder, silvery hair caught in the black fabric, and she was staring at nothing in particular. Her pretty mouth was soft and vulnerable, her cheeks still very pale. He remembered the bright smiles she always had for him, the joy that had lit her expression whenever he'd visited, and now...

Now she looked defeated, all the brightness, all the joy, gone.

You did that to her.

He had. And so he'd fix it.

'You didn't fail,' he said flatly. 'What happened in the ballroom was my fault and mine alone.'

She looked up at him, frowning. 'What do you mean, it's your fault? You're not the one who forgot everyone's name or knocked a glass out of—'

'No, but I'm the one who ignored you the entire week, giving your preparation over to someone else who clearly had no idea what they were doing. I'm the one who didn't check on you to make sure things were running smoothly. And I'm the one who didn't ask you tonight if you felt prepared or take any notice of how pale you were or how frightened you looked.' He stared into her reddened eyes, wanting her to be absolutely certain. 'It won't happen again. Do you understand?'

Her cheeks had gained a little colour, which was good. 'Did I really look that frightened?'

'Yes. You looked terrified.'

Her silvery lashes descended, veiling her gaze. 'I didn't mean to. I'm…not very good at hiding my emotions.'

'You'll learn. But not in a week.' He came to

the doors of his private apartments, the guards rushing to open them so he could walk through. 'And, given that for the last five years you've been living in the country with no court experience at all, it was unconscionable for me to expect this of you so quickly.'

'You don't need to blame yourself,' she said quietly. 'Some of this was my fault too. It reminded me too much of all those parties my mother kept dragging me to and I suppose I… panicked.'

He knew what her mother had put her through. She'd told him, in the months after their wedding, when he'd visited her, how her parents had never been happy with her and how she'd always disappointed them.

He hadn't realised, though, that balls and social engagements would still be an issue, even all these years later.

You should have.

Yes, damn right he should have.

'No, it was not.' He couldn't bear for her to take the blame, not even a small part of it. 'I'm the King, and you're my queen, therefore it's my responsibility to prepare you for your role.

And I should have remembered that about your mother.'

His footsteps echoed on the marble floor as he passed by the door of his study, carrying on down towards his bedroom.

Because that was where this had to end.

It was his own desires that had got Inara tangled up in this, so it would be his own desires that he'd deal with first. And perhaps, once he had, he could then focus on the important work of preparing her to undertake her queenly duties properly.

He was conscious of Inara's gaze on him as he walked, of her warm body in his arms and how it seemed to fit there perfectly. Of how his hunger seemed to grow with each step and how his anticipation gathered tighter and tighter.

'I didn't think it would be such an issue for me, so why you should have been able to anticipate it I have no idea,' she murmured. 'You don't have to take responsibility for everything, you know.'

He didn't deign to respond. Of course he had to take responsibility for everything. He was the King. What else did a king do?

But it was becoming difficult to think of anything beyond the feel of her in his arms, and how he hadn't been able to look at her all evening. Yet now, in the privacy of his bedroom, he'd strip that gown from her body and look his fill.

No one will be watching you. No one will be judging you.

His breath caught as realisation gripped him tight.

In his bedroom he could be anyone he wanted. There'd be no one to see him. No one to know if his crown slipped a little, or even a lot.

No one but Inara. And she already knew who he truly was inside. She always had.

'Where are we going, Cassius?' She sounded as if she already knew.

He glanced down once more, meeting her gaze. 'Where we should have gone the night you arrived. To my bedroom.'

CHAPTER SEVEN

INARA'S HEART WAS beating very fast. The awful, sick feeling in her stomach and the tightness in her chest that she'd felt in the ballroom had vanished, both feelings melting away as soon as Cassius's arms came around her, holding her tight.

The evening had started awfully the moment Cassius had led her into the ballroom, and from there it had gone from awful to terrible, then to even worse. She hadn't been able to remember anyone's names, and her attempts at conversation had only prompted frowns, strange looks and judgmental stares. No one had been friendly. No one had smiled. Everything the etiquette people had taught her had gone completely out of her head and she'd felt paralyzed, certain that the moment she opened her mouth she'd only make it worse.

She hadn't wanted to move, in case she'd tried to curtsey instead of shaking hands or stood accidentally on someone's foot. Her eyes had been sore because the contact lenses were irritating, and her head had hurt because the pins in her hair were digging into her scalp. She wasn't used to wearing the tall silver heels they'd given her to wear, either—they'd made her feel as if she were wearing a pair of stilts.

And through it all, his arm like iron beneath her fingertips, had moved Cassius. Tall and broad, as unreachable and untouchable as Mount Everest. She'd wanted to impress him so badly, yet every time she'd opened her mouth or taken a step she'd made some mistake. And he'd seen. He'd watched her fail, fail and fail.

Failing her parents was one thing, but failing him was quite another.

It cut her to the bone.

He'd lost his family, had had to pick up a duty he'd never asked for, and the least she could do for him was to give him a queen he could be proud of.

But then she'd knocked that woman's elbow and wine had gone everywhere, splashing her beautiful dress and causing a scene. Reminding her of that garden party years ago, when she'd tried her best to catch the eye of the duke's son, only to stammer and forget every rule of conversation the instant he'd spoken to her. She'd been so embarrassed that she'd run away.

Back then she'd been young, only sixteen, yet tonight she'd had no such excuse. She was now an adult and a queen, and she should have stayed in the ballroom and dealt with the mess she'd made, not bolted like a frightened rabbit.

In fact, she'd been on the point of mustering her courage to go back when Cassius had appeared. Everything in her had tightened as she'd braced herself for his judgment and then…it hadn't come.

He'd seemed angry, coming over to where she'd sat on the cold stone bench, his gaze full of fire. But he hadn't given her a tirade. Instead, he'd shocked her by draping his jacket around her shoulders then picking her straight up in his arms.

And it had come as another shock to realise that he was only angry with himself. He'd taken responsibility for the entire evening.

That shouldn't have surprised her. He'd assumed a duty he'd never wanted, becoming king because of a tragic accident. It had always puzzled her that he'd done that because, although he had been next in line to the throne, he hadn't had to take it. There were others he could have handed the responsibility on to, yet he hadn't. Some would have said it was power he was after, but Inara knew he wasn't that kind of man. He never had been.

So why did he take it?

But she didn't have an answer to that and, with his sharp, intense gaze on her, the question began to fray and break apart.

She was in his arms in her glittering, wine-soaked dress, after having made a fool of herself in front of his entire court, and yet instead of yelling at her he'd told her it was his fault and now he was carrying her into his bedroom...

'Why?' The question came out breathily as he strode into the room, kicking the door shut behind him. 'You changed your mind when I first arrived, so why now?'

He moved over to the tall stone fireplace, a blaze leaping in the grate. It looked as though it had been freshly lit, and she was aware all of a sudden that she'd been cold sitting in the pavilion. Yet she wasn't cold now. His arms were strong, his hard chest like hot stone. His jacket around her shoulders was warm too, and it smelled of him, a masculine spice with an earthier scent that was all Cassius.

Her mouth went dry, a bone-deep, physical longing curling through her. It was very hard to think about what had happened earlier and her own conflicted feelings when he was here, he was holding her and it was very apparent what he intended to do.

Gently, he put her down in front of the fire, which quite frankly felt like a crime when she wanted to stay in his arms and never leave.

'Because I thought it best to give you some time to become accustomed to palace life.' He moved behind her, easing his jacket from her shoulders.

Inara shivered as his fingertips brushed her bare skin, the physical longing becoming deeper and more insistent. It was getting difficult to think, and part of her just wanted to surrender, to let the desire overtake her, because she'd done nothing but think all night and she was tired of it. She wanted to escape. Numbers had always been that escape, but it wasn't the stark purity of numbers she wanted now. She only wanted him.

Except…he wasn't giving her the entire truth, was he? He'd changed his mind so abruptly that day in his study after making all those grand proclamations. Why? It wasn't simply because he wanted to give her some time to adjust, she was sure. He'd walked away from her so quickly after she'd got close to him…

'No,' she said huskily, staring at the flames leaping high in the fireplace, every sense concentrated on the man standing behind her, on the heat of his body and the scent of him that wrapped around her, making her feel so safe, the way it always had. 'That's not the reason.'

His fingers moved in her hair, carefully extracting each painful pin. 'The reason doesn't matter.'

Her hair began to come down, slipping over her shoulders, her scalp aching in relief as he pulled away the tiara, dropping it onto a nearby armchair.

'Yes, it does.' She shivered as his fingers wound into her hair, combing through it. 'At least, it matters to me. You could have come for me any time this week and you didn't.'

'The time wasn't right.'

Inara turned, looking up into his familiar, achingly beautiful face. He was so very tall, built so broad, so muscular. A warrior who could crush her without even thinking. But he wouldn't. All that magnificent male strength was tightly leashed, so painstakingly controlled.

Everything about him was so painstakingly controlled.

He didn't used to be, remember? He used to be much more relaxed, so much...happier.

Yet there was nothing of the man he'd once been in his face. The duties of kingship had stripped it all away, taking that happiness with it.

Her heart ached with a sudden, painful realisation. She'd never thought much about him as a man. He'd always been a fantasy figure, a template on which she could hang her own longings and desires.

But he wasn't a template. He wasn't even a king—that was only a title. First and foremost, he was a man, and a complicated one at that.

She stared up into his level amber gaze. 'It's not about timing. You changed your mind very suddenly that night and then you left me alone for an entire week. You didn't even respond to the messages I sent you.'

The expression on his face was set, and he radiated tension like the fire behind him radiated warmth, yet in his eyes were flames hotter than those in the grate.

She could feel herself begin to catch fire too, though she resisted the pull. This was too important, like the key to solving an equation she'd been studying and hadn't found a solution to yet.

'Turn around, little one,' Cassius ordered, his voice very deep, his gaze turning from smoky amber into brilliant, burning gold. 'The time for talking is over.'

Her whole body tightened with the need to obey him but she knew, if she did, if she let this moment pass, it would set a precedent for their marriage that would be difficult to depart from.

He'd told her he didn't see her as a child any more, but even so he was still treating her like one. He was the one in charge, telling her what to do, where to go, that this was how it should be, and she'd accepted it. And not simply because he was her king, but because she'd so badly wanted his approval.

He'd taken control, but only because she'd let him.

And you'll always be a child to him as long as you keep doing so.

Determination hardened inside her. If she continued to fall in with his wishes, to accept it every time he said no, then things would never change between them. He would continue to view her as his child bride, and their marriage would simply be an endless set of orders she obeyed, while he got to dictate everything.

Well, that ended tonight.

'The time for talking is not over.' Inara lifted her chin. 'If you want me, Cassius, you need to tell me the truth.'

The flames in his eyes glowed brighter. 'Are you trying to bargain with your king?'

His voice was calm, yet there was an edge to it, a note of warning that sent a small electric thrill through her, excitement gathering in her throat.

The growing intensity in him was making it harder to resist, but this mattered. She couldn't let it go.

'Maybe,' she said, her breathing getting faster.

'You can't bargain with me, little one.' His hands settled on her shoulders and gripped her gently but firmly, the heat of his touch stealing all the breath from her lungs. Then he turned her round so she faced the fire once more, with him at her back. 'Kings take what they want. And they don't accept bargains.'

Anticipation coiled low inside her, bringing with it a nagging, insistent ache. Tension crackled in the air around them, not the same tension that seemed to be holding him back, but something else. Something hot and electric. She'd felt it that night in the study, when he'd teased her, flirted with her, and she'd challenged him. He'd liked that then and she was sure he liked it now.

Maybe that was the key to unlocking him. Maybe she should take this further, play this game and see where it led. Maybe she'd get the truth out of him, and some power and respect for herself.

'They don't?' She hoped she sounded more in control than she felt. 'Surely if it was in this king's interest he might?'

'In my interest, hmm?' His thumbs stroked over her bare shoulders, searing her skin, sending delicious chills through her. 'And what have you got to bargain with?'

Inara closed her eyes, every sense focused on the man at her back and, despite the fact that he towered over her, all hard, masculine strength and power, she'd never felt so safe.

Yet at the same time she knew she was also in danger. Danger of the most exciting kind.

'Tell me why you sent me away,' she said huskily, 'and I'll let you do anything you want to me. Anything at all. You won't need to ask. You can just take.'

Cassius stilled. Her skin beneath his fingers was soft, and very, very warm, and he felt like a starving beast he was so hungry.

He took a breath, then another, trying to focus on what she'd just said, because she couldn't mean it. She couldn't. She was small and delicate and very innocent. Too innocent. She couldn't mean what he thought she meant.

'You don't want that,' he said roughly. 'You don't know what you're—'

'I know exactly what I'm offering.' She sounded almost…cool. As if she was the one with the control here, not him. 'And I mean it, too. You can have me, all of me, for as long as you want, doing anything you want. I give you permission right now. All I want in return is for you to be honest with me.'

Her shoulders beneath his hand felt narrow and fragile, and yet the heat coming off her…

She was hotter than the fire in front of them. And she smelled of sex and sin and all the things he'd denied himself. All the things he could have right now in the privacy of his own bedroom. No one to watch him. No one to see if he let himself be just a man for a few hours. Just for tonight. Just with her. She was his wife, after all. It was allowed.

Except she wouldn't allow it unless he gave her the truth. He hadn't expected her to want to know. He hadn't expected her to be interested. What he'd expected was her complete surrender, the way she'd surrendered to him in the library that night. The way she'd surrendered out in the pavilion overlooking the sea, letting him scoop her into his arms.

He hadn't expected her to question him or to hold out when he'd told her not to. He hadn't expected her to push him.

The predator he'd once been growled low and hungry, liking this challenge to his authority. Liking her determination too, because he'd never been a fan of a pushover. He preferred women who knew what they wanted and weren't afraid to say it. And it had been a long time since anyone had challenged him like this, because no one challenged the King.

Except, clearly, his queen.

'Why are you so interested?' He brushed aside the silvery mass of her hair, baring her nape before bending and pressing a kiss there. 'I've given you the answer to your question.'

She shivered. 'What you gave me was an excuse. And now you're making this into a big deal.'

She's not wrong.

He pressed another kiss to the top of her spine, inhaling the sweet scent of her body. His hunger was becoming more and more difficult to contain. The restraints he'd put on himself were starting to fray. If he hadn't already given himself permission, it might have worried him, but he had given himself permission, and now all he felt was impatience.

Yes, he was making this into a big deal. What did it matter if she knew that she was the reason he'd kept his distance this week? It gave her a certain power over him that he was reluctant to let her have but, whether she knew it yet or not, she was already using that power over him right now, right here, in this room. And it was working.

Cassius had never taken a woman without permission, even when he'd been at his worst, and he certainly wasn't about to start now, so he murmured in her ear, 'Why did I change my mind that night? Why did I keep my distance all week? I think you know why already, little one.'

He took hold of the zip of her gown. 'It was you. I changed my mind because of you. Because I want you. Because a good king is controlled and measured in all things and you make me forget that. You make me remember who I used to be and I cannot have that.'

Slowly he began to draw down the zip, the silvery fabric parting to reveal silky pale skin and the elegant curve of her back. She made no move to stop him, but he could feel her tremble. 'But…why? Why can't you remember who you used to be? What's so bad about that?'

He didn't want to get into that. Didn't want to tell her the bitter truth about himself and how flawed he was. How he'd sent his own brother, his twin, to his death.

He never wanted to tell *anyone* about that.

So he unzipped her gown all the way and

pushed it from her body, letting it fall at her feet in a pool of glittering wine-soaked fabric, leaving her wearing nothing but lacy underwear and silver high heels.

'Cassius,' she murmured, her voice sounding slightly uncertain.

He put his hands on her hips, drawing her back against his body and holding her there. 'Not now,' he said quietly in her ear. 'I gave you what you wanted. It's my turn now.' Then he turned his head, brushing his mouth over the sensitive place between her shoulder and neck before biting her there lightly.

She gasped, so he bit her again, sliding his hands slowly and with care up her sides and then back down again, tracing the glorious feminine shape of her.

Delicate and finely made, his queen. She hadn't yet become sharp and rigid and unbending, as he had. She was still hot and soft, like candle wax melting so beautifully under his touch. There was passion in his bride, so much of it, and she was going to give it all to him.

It was a gift, and he knew it. And not just her passion, but her trust too. Anything, she'd told him. He could do anything to her and she'd let him....

He nipped her again, gently, then dropped to his knees behind her, pressing kisses down her spine as his hands went to her hips, his fingers slipping under the waistband of her knickers. She gave a trembling sigh as he eased them down her legs to her ankles, helping her to step out of them and the miles of tulle of her gown. Then he swept the clothing aside so she stood free and unencumbered, naked but for the sexy silver heels.

She began to turn, but he gripped her, keeping her right where she was. 'No. Stay still.'

Then he ran his palms down the outsides of her thighs to her knees, and then down further, tracing her calves and then her ankles. He could hear her breathing, fast and erratic, and she kept shifting on her feet. He stroked her again, from her ankles up to her hips then back down again, glorying in the feel of her skin. It had been so long since he'd touched a woman...

He frowned at her feet and the backs of her heels where the leather of her shoes had obviously rubbed, turning the skin red. 'Are your feet sore?'

'Only a little,' she said breathlessly. 'I'm not... used to heels.'

Another reminder if he needed one that tonight must have been a nightmare for her, and that he'd let it happen.

But he'd fix it. Right now, right here, he'd make it better, the way he used to, by giving her the only good thing he was capable of: pleasure.

'You're unbelievably sexy in those heels,' he murmured, running his hands up her legs once more, pressing kisses to the small of her back. 'But I can't have them hurting you.'

'Oh, it's okay. I don't mind. Not if you like them.'

'I do like them. But I also mind that they're hurting you.' Sitting back on his heels, he closed his hand around one delicate ankle and lifted it, easing the shoe off, before doing the same to her other foot. Then he knelt there and began to touch her body, outlining every dip and curve with his fingertips. The narrow indentation of her waist and the soft roundness of her bottom. The sweet swell of hips and thighs. The delicate arcs of her shoulder blades and the graceful curve of her neck.

She shook as he traced her, but he didn't rush

it. He wanted to take his time, because if he was going to allow himself a whole night to indulge in her…with permission to do whatever he wanted…then he was going to make the most of it.

His hunger simmered as he fed it small bites. The velvet of the back of her neck. The petal softness in the crook of her elbow. The creamy taste of the small of her back as he pressed his tongue there.

Her breathing became louder and more erratic as he went on, and she leaned against him, as if she couldn't hold herself upright any longer. But he'd only just started, and he wasn't done with her yet, not even close.

When he'd explored every inch of her from behind, he turned her round to face him at last, staying on his knees because he wanted to savour her up close.

And what a sight she was, her pretty face flushed with heat, her silvery-grey eyes darkening into charcoal. She had the most perfect round, pink-tipped breasts, and the soft curls between her thighs were as silvery as the hair on her head.

His breath caught at the sight of her, the simmering hunger beginning to boil. He was so hard and so ready, but his long years of self-control had taught him well so, instead of picking her up and throwing her on the bed the way his sex was demanding, he stayed where he was, put his hands on her hips and drew her closer.

She reached for him, swaying on her feet, clutching at his shoulders, her gaze open and so full of longing and heat that for a second every thought went straight out of his head.

He'd seen an echo of that look before, every time he'd visited her. When she'd come rushing into the room to greet him, her face lit up, eyes shining. And it hit him all of a sudden that she'd been the brightest part of those years before his family had died.

He'd thought he was happy then, rebelling against his rigid upbringing and all the palace rules. Throwing them in his father's face and indulging himself whenever and wherever he could.

But he hadn't been happy. He'd been at war with his family…at war with the ideals that he felt had been forced on him…at war with his place in the world. He'd been living selfishly and a part of him knew it.

Really, the only time he'd ever felt true happiness was when he'd come to visit her. When she'd smiled at him, taking him out of his own petty grievances and pain. Distracting him, teaching him what it was to be interested in another person, not just himself.

He'd married her because of the way she'd looked at him that night in his limo, seeing in him something better, something worthy. A hero. A saviour. And that was how she'd continued to see him, no matter how awful or selfish he'd been. No matter how imperfect. No matter how flawed.

She saw the good in him and it gave him hope.

She wasn't smiling now, but that same look was glowing in her eyes, only this time it was hotter and tinged with passion. And suddenly he was almost beside himself with desperation. To touch her, taste her, explore every part of her. Take her out of herself, the way she'd done to him.

To feel like he was worthy.

He pulled her closer, pressing his mouth to her stomach, licking her and then moving higher to take one of those little pink nipples into his mouth. She tasted so sweet, like strawberries and champagne from a long-lost summer, and when she groaned, arching into him, offering herself, she sounded even sweeter.

He was starving, desperate for her. Releasing her breast, he licked his way down her over her stomach to the soft, sensitive place between her thighs. She gasped as he nuzzled against her damp curls and then, when he slid his hands over the curves of her bottom to hold her steady, sliding his tongue through her slick folds, she cried out.

She was delicious, the best thing he'd tasted in his entire life, and he couldn't get enough. She sagged against him, folding herself over him, panting out her pleasure, saying his name like a prayer as he explored all the delicate textures of her, silken, slick and hot.

And, as he lost himself in her, he had the oddest feeling that it was her sheltering him, her holding him up, rather than the other way around.

He wanted to hold her there for ever, forgetting everything but the sound of her cries and the taste of her on his tongue. But her pleasure was a double-edged sword, because her every cry sharpened his own hunger until he couldn't stand it any more. He pushed his tongue deep inside her, gripping her hard as she cried out his name and convulsed in his arms.

He stayed where he was through sheer will power alone, holding her as she quietened. Only then did he rise to his feet, sweeping her into his arms and carrying her over to the bed.

Then he laid her on it and followed her down, putting one hand on either side of her head, stretching himself over her.

He looked down into her darkened eyes, tendrils of silver hair clinging to her damp forehead.

'Time to make good on your bargain, little one,' he growled.

CHAPTER EIGHT

INARA COULDN'T THINK of anywhere she'd rather be than right here, in Cassius's bed, beneath him, his gaze gone brilliant with hunger and desire, and all for her.

Yes, *her.*

She'd wondered why he'd kept his distance and, even though she'd shied away from thinking about it, some deep part of her had doubted. Doubted that, despite his lapse in the library at the Queen's Estate, it hadn't been about *her.* That it was just because he hadn't had a woman in years. That he didn't really want her after all.

It hadn't been something she'd wanted to admit even to herself, though, so she'd deliberately pushed it away. The way he'd carried her into his bedroom had relieved her somewhat, but the deeper doubt had remained.

Until he'd given her the truth. She *was* the reason he'd kept his distance. Not because he didn't want her, but because he did. Too much.

You make me remember how I used to be.

That admission troubled her, caught at her, made her want to know more. Because there had been something conflicted in his voice, as if remembering who he used to be was a bad thing. As if he *wasn't* that person any more and was now someone different.

He is different. He changed when he became king.

He had. He'd become so distant, so…not cold, precisely, but chilly. As if there were oceans between him and everyone else. She'd assumed that was just part of being a king, but maybe it wasn't. Maybe there was something more to it.

Except it was difficult to think of that now, with him crouched over her like a beast, his brilliant, hungry gaze on hers.

Aftershocks of pleasure still jolted through her. After the intense climax he'd given her with his mouth right there in front of the fire, she'd thought it wasn't possible to be ready for another so soon. How wrong she was. The way he looked at her, as if he wanted to eat her alive, made her whole body tighten with need and desire.

'Anything,' she said thickly, staring up at him,

meeting his fierce stare with her own. 'You can have anything. I promised and I meant it.'

She *did* mean it. She'd never been so sure of anything in her life. She had no experience whatsoever, not like he did, but that didn't matter. He'd keep her safe. She knew that on an almost cellular level. There was nothing he could do to her that she wouldn't want, nothing that she wouldn't enjoy.

She wasn't afraid of him or what he might to do her in the slightest.

It's not your body you should be worried about. It's your heart.

The thought was a cold thread cutting through the heat, and she didn't want it there, so she ignored it.

That didn't matter—not here, not right now.

Slowly Cassius straightened, still watching her with that hungry amber gaze. He lifted his hands to the buttons of his shirt and began to undo them, slowly, teasing her, and she loved it—the slow reveal of his bare chest as the cotton parted, letting her see at last the hard, ridged lines of his chest and abdomen, sharply defined, as though he'd been chiselled from rock by a master sculptor.

She pushed herself up, hungry to touch him, but almost as soon as she put her hands on his hot, smooth skin he grabbed her wrists and pushed her back down against the mattress.

'No.' His voice was rough and guttural. 'Not yet.'

'Oh, but I—'

'You'll get your turn, I promise. But I'm too hungry for you to do that right now. My self-control isn't limitless where you're concerned.'

She loved that too. That she really *could* test him. That his desire for her was apparently just as hungry as hers was for him. It made her feel strong, a current of unexpected power running through her. That she, the failure, the girl her parents had never particularly wanted, could tempt a king.

She wanted to tease him the way he was teasing her, so she gave him what she hoped was a flirtatious look from beneath her lashes. 'Hurry up then, Your Majesty. I'm getting impatient.'

Then she wondered if she'd done something wrong, because he stared at her for a few seconds with that blank expression she was beginning to think was his default when he was shocked. But, just as a flush of embarrassment threatened, his beautiful, sensual mouth curled in the most devastating smile she'd ever seen.

He'd never smiled like that at her. In fact, it had been three years since she'd seen him smile, full-stop.

Her heart twisted, giving one hard, desperate beat, and she swore in that moment that, if nothing else, she'd spend the rest of their marriage trying to make him smile like that again. No—she'd dedicate her entire life to it. He was so beautiful when he smiled. Warm and wicked and unbelievably sexy. No wonder he'd had a never-ending stream of women all queuing for a night in his bed.

'Are you perhaps teasing me, little one?' His voice was low and rough, a velvet growl.

'Maybe.' She felt triumphant, as if she'd won a Nobel prize. 'Though it's not the done thing, is it? To tease a king?'

Cassius shrugged out of his shirt and let it fall, his hands dropping to the belt on his trousers. 'No, it's not. Kings are very serious and hate being teased.' He began to unfasten his belt. 'There are laws, you know. And consequences.'

Inara was thrilled. Who'd have thought that she'd love flirting? Because that was what they were doing, wasn't it? They were flirting. And, unlike that night in the library when she'd been so uncertain, she wasn't uncertain now. Not when it was clear he was enjoying this as much as she was.

'Consequences?' She took in his hard-muscled torso before focusing on what his hands were doing with his belt—undoing it, pulling it from the belt loops and discarding it. 'What kind of consequences are there for teasing a king?'

He pulled down the zip of his fly. 'Give me five minutes and I'll show you.'

'Five minutes?' Inara's mouth went dry as he shifted on the bed, pushing his trousers down and taking his underwear with them. 'Is that all?'

Cassius laughed, roughly, deeply and unbelievably sexily. 'Not a response I'm familiar with, I have to say.'

Inara blinked, staring at that most male part of him, all flirtatious banter instantly going out of her head. Back in the library she hadn't had a chance to see him properly, hadn't even had a chance to touch him, but now... Oh, now...

'I didn't mean th-that,' she stuttered, sitting up as he got off the bed to get rid of the rest of his clothes, then reaching for him as he came back, stretching himself out over her. 'I meant…'

'I know.' He caught her wrists once again and put them down on either side of her head as he eased his big, muscled body between her thighs. 'Time to stop talking now.'

And, before she could say another word, his mouth was on hers, hot and demanding, ravaging her mouth. She tried to kiss him back, but he gave her no quarter, conquering her so completely that she simply surrendered, letting him take whatever he wanted.

Then his hands were sliding beneath her, lifting her hips, and she felt him thrust into her, a long, deep slide that made her cry out in pleasure.

It was different from before. Then, she'd been on top of him, his hands on her hips gripping her so that, even though they had been joined, there had been a distance between them.

Now, there was no distance. She was surrounded by him, by his heat and his scent, by the rough sounds of his ragged breathing and the exquisite friction of him moving inside her. There was no pain now and no awkwardness or uncertainty. Only a growing intensity, a longing that gripped her as tightly as he did.

She put her hands on his powerful shoulders, feeling the flex and release of hard muscle, the strength in him a wild thrill she'd never imagined. And she hung on, wanting to get closer, even closer than they were already, because it wasn't enough.

'C-Cassius.' His name was both a hoarse prayer and a plea, though for what she had no idea.

But it was clear that he knew, because his mouth was on hers again, kissing her as he moved, driving her relentlessly towards the edge a second time.

Then everything began to fray around the edges, pleasure blooming inside her like the most intricate and elegant of equations, the solution to it so, so close. So very, very close...

It was him, wasn't it? *He* was the solution. *He* was the answer to every question, every problem, every difficulty she'd ever had. It was him.

It had always been him.

Inara wrapped her arms around his neck, desperate to hold onto him, unable to escape the feeling that, once this was over, she'd lose him.

That this sexy, wicked man would slip away, turning once more into a king.

But nothing was going to stop the climax from happening and, when he slipped his hand between her thighs, stroking her gently, she could feel herself break, shattering like a fragile piece of glass thrown onto a tiled floor.

She sobbed as the pleasure overwhelmed her and she broke apart. She was only dimly aware of him letting go of the leash on himself, slamming into her hard, fast and out of rhythm, until she felt his teeth against her shoulder, a growl of pleasure escaping him as the climax came for him too.

For a while after that, time drifted and Inara let herself simply lie in his arms, enjoying having him so close, holding her, his body pressed the length of hers, his breath ghosting over her skin. She lay underneath him, safe and protected by his strength, and there was nowhere else she wanted to be.

Right now, he wasn't distant or chilly. He wasn't the King. He wasn't even wicked Prince Cassius, scourge of the bedrooms of Europe. He was just Cassius, her lover, another side of him that she'd newly discovered. Another part of him that she'd fallen in love with.

She let out a soft breath.

Perhaps this marriage would work. Perhaps it would be okay. During the day he might be a distant king, and she'd have to concentrate hard on learning how to be his queen. But all that would be bearable if she could have Cassius, her lover, at night.

If they had this, then surely she didn't need anything else?

Finally, he stirred, lifting his head and looking down at her, examining her critically. Then he smiled that devastating smile again, the one that set her heart racing and her pulse sky-rocketing.

'You said I could do anything to you, didn't you?' Desire burned in his gaze.

Inara swallowed, feeling that longing for him begin all over again. 'Yes.'

'Good.' Then he flipped her over onto her stomach and covered her with his body.

Cassius kept Inara up most of the night, sating his pleasure and hers in as many ways as he could think of which, considering the wide breadth of his experience, was quite a few. Eventually she fell into an exhausted sleep and he let her, though he didn't sleep himself.

He was content to hold her, aware of nothing but how good her warm, silky body felt against his, and how calming he found the soft, regular sound of her breathing. It was good, too, to think of nothing. To be nothing more in this bed than a man holding a woman.

But as dawn came he knew he couldn't afford to stay being a mere man, that he would have to be King again in a few short hours, and he couldn't prepare himself adequately for that while she was in his arms.

So he shifted without waking her, slipping from the bed and pulling on his trousers, moving out of the bedroom and walking down the stone corridors to his study.

The first rays of morning light were shining through the windows, the sound of the sea wild outside.

It was his morning ritual to tend to his plants. It calmed his mind and settled him for the day ahead, allowing him to put aside his own petty concerns and feelings and to become the king he needed to be.

It usually worked.

But this morning he couldn't concentrate. His mind was too full of Inara and the memories of the night before. Of her skin beneath his hands and the delicate scent of her arousal. Of her cries and sobs of pleasure and the husky way she'd said his name. The way she had made good on her promise, letting him do whatever he wanted to her, and clearly loving every moment of it. There had been no fear in her, only absolute trust. It had shone in her eyes so brightly, it made something in his chest ache.

He didn't deserve it. He'd married her because it had made him feel good that she'd looked at him as if he was her saviour, not out of any real concern for her, and then, apart from a few visits, he'd forgotten about her. For years. Then he'd tried to get rid of her with a divorce, only reluctantly agreeing to stay married when circumstances had forced him to…

But that's you all over, isn't it? You only take responsibility when you're forced to.

Cassius gritted his teeth, trying to get his thoughts under control as he examined the small azalea he was in the process of sculpting.

He shouldn't be thinking about this. He should be thinking about the day ahead and the things he had to do, not his own personal failings—of which there were many, naturally, but he didn't let them get in the way of his job.

He'd dedicated the last three years of his life to *not* doing that.

But aren't you doing it again? Letting her get to you?

Cassius snipped off a small branch. No, a delay in settling his thoughts was *not* letting her get to him. Another half an hour and he'd be fine. He wouldn't think of her again for the rest of the day.

She needs more guidance. What are you going to do? Ignore her for another week? Sabotage her chances of being the kind of queen you wanted?

Without thinking, Cassius snipped off another branch, realising only at the last minute that it wasn't one he'd meant to cut. Muttering a filthy curse, he tried to haul his mind back to the task at hand and not let it get distracted by Inara, but then he heard the sound of the door opening then closing behind him.

He didn't turn. He knew who'd come in. He could smell her warm scent getting closer, making his body harden instantly.

'What are you doing in here?' Inara asked.

He wanted very much to drop his scissors, turn round and take her back to bed to replay some of his favourite memories from the night before, but it was morning. A new day. And in an hour or two his presence would be required and he would need to act like a king instead of a hormonal teenage boy. He'd have to explain his abrupt absence from the ball the night before, for a start.

'I'm preparing myself for the day,' he said, without looking around. 'Go back to bed, little one.'

Inara ignored him, coming closer, and then a small, warm hand rested lightly on the bare skin of his back.

'What kind of tree is that?' she asked curiously, peering at the azalea on the shelf in front of him. 'It's very pretty.'

Every thought went straight out of his head. All he could think about was her hand on his skin and how it made him burn. How it made him want. As if all the desires he'd successfully managed to contain for years were in danger of bursting out.

She's put a crack in your control.

No, that wasn't true. He hadn't been at all controlled the night before, admittedly, but that had been purposeful. He'd consciously put being a king aside and let himself be a man for once.

He could put the man aside at any time. It wasn't a problem. Still, he shifted minutely, causing her hand to drop away. His attention was on the tree, but he could feel the surprise radiating from her. He told himself he didn't feel the warmth lingering on his skin from her casual touch.

A silence fell.

Cassius made another precise snip with the scissors.

'You're him again, aren't you?' Inara's voice was very quiet.

He examined the cut he'd made. 'Him? What do you mean?'

'You're the King again.'

'I'm always the King.' He ignored the thread of what sounded like disappointment in her voice. 'I don't stop being him.'

'But you never wanted to be. You told me your brother was welcome to the job. That you'd rather die than have it.'

He remembered that conversation, over a

long and leisurely lunch at the townhouse she'd lived in before he'd ascended the throne. She'd asked him in her usual blunt, curious way about whether he was disappointed at being younger than his brother by a few minutes and whether he'd ever want to be King.

'Caspian is welcome to it. Personally, I'd rather die than have the job.'

A throwaway comment. Such a careless remark, when a year later…

It should have been you. You're the one who should have died. But you didn't. It was your brother who took your place, the way he always did.

Everything in him went tight and sharp and hot, and before he could stop himself he said, 'Yes, well, as it turned out it wasn't me who died. Caspian took that honour and I got the job anyway.'

He hadn't meant to sound so bitter and as soon as the words were out he wished he hadn't said them. They revealed too much. But it was too late and he knew it.

In the echoing silence he could feel her looking at him. He didn't look back, concentrating on the tree instead.

'Why did you take it, Cassius?'

He didn't want to talk about this, not when he had less than an hour before he had to be in his office. So he couldn't understand why he answered her. 'Because there was no one else.'

'But didn't you have a cousin somewhere? Couldn't she have taken the throne?'

This had to stop.

He dropped the scissors and turned.

Inara was standing right next to him, her silvery hair loose down her back, and she was wearing his shirt from the night before. It was far too big for her, the sleeves rolled up hugely, the hem almost reaching her knees.

It should have looked ridiculous. Instead, she was so indescribably beautiful it made his chest hurt and that primitive, possessive thing inside him growl with satisfaction.

She wore his shirt and she smelled like him. *Yours.*

Oh, yes, she was. Which made this battle with himself and his desires pointless, an old pattern of behaviour he didn't need, not now. She was his wife; she was living with him; she'd be in his bed every night. Which meant that, while during the day he had to be the King, at night he didn't. He could be himself. And it wasn't losing self-control. It was only sex, only relaxing after a hard day's work. After all, every other person on the planet did it; why couldn't a king?

'No,' he said. 'My cousin couldn't take the throne because it was my responsibility.' He put the scissors back on the shelf. 'A throne isn't like any other job, Inara. It's a duty. You can't just decide not to do it because it's too hard or you don't like the work. It's not about *you* at all. It's about the role, the responsibility you have to your subjects.'

Her brow wrinkled. She had her glasses on again and her luminous grey eyes seemed less red. Clearly the contacts she'd been wearing had irritated her eyes. He made a mental note to let the stylist know that the Queen preferred glasses. He should never have made her wear contacts.

'But Aveiras didn't want you,' she pointed out bluntly. 'You could have passed it on to someone else and they would have been fine with it.'

A formless anger simmered inside him, an anger he hadn't been aware of before, and yet it tasted familiar. As if it had been there all this time.

'Careful,' he said. 'Be very careful what you say.'

'Why?' She looked stubborn, determination glittering in her eyes. 'Does no one ever talk to you about these things? Does no one ever question you?'

'No, they don't.' The anger twined with the embers of his desire, creating something hotter, more demanding. 'I'm the King.'

'Actually,' Inara said, 'I'm beginning to wonder if you're not so much a king as a world-class martyr.'

Something jolted hard inside him, as if she'd struck him, and the simmering anger and desire began to boil over.

Cassius reached for her, pulling her hard up against him. 'Don't push it, Inara,' he growled. 'I'm not the Prince any more. You can't—'

'Well, you should be.' She stared at him as if he was no threat to her whatsoever. As if his anger was nothing. As if he was just a normal man she was arguing with and not the leader of an entire nation. 'At least that prince was honest with himself. He didn't nail himself to the cross of duty like you're doing right now.'

'Of course he didn't,' Cassius ground out before he could stop himself. 'Because that prince hadn't yet killed his brother.'

Inara's pretty mouth opened in a soft O of surprise, her eyes going wide. Her hands were on his chest, her palms like hot coals on his bare skin. 'What? What do you mean, he hadn't killed his brother?'

Let her go. Walk away.

He should. But the anger needed to do that had gone, leaving in its place only a burning desire to tell someone. He'd kept it a secret for so long, a heavy weight he'd been dragging around for years, and he was tired of it. So very tired. And he had no one else to tell. A king didn't have friends or confidantes; a king had no one but himself and his own secrets. But his secrets were eating him alive.

So who better to tell than the person who knew him better than anyone else? The person he'd always been honest with, always himself?

'Caspian wasn't supposed to be on the helicopter that day,' he said roughly. 'I was. But I made him swap places with me because I had a hangover and I didn't want to go.'

Shock rippled over Inara's lovely face. 'Oh, Cassius.'

He didn't know what kind of response he wanted from her, but it wasn't the pity he heard in her voice. She shouldn't pity him. She should be horrified. Not only because of how he'd sent his brother to his death, but his parents as well.

He let her go. Suddenly, he didn't want her warmth near him, touching him. Reminding him of all the things he couldn't allow himself to have. Because he didn't deserve it, not any of it.

'The trip to the mountains that day was my fault too.' He stripped the emotion completely from his voice so all that was left was the truth. 'My father was displeased with my behaviour and wanted me to see the tombs of the de Leon kings so I was aware of the legacy I was supposed to uphold. I hated all the rules I was supposed to obey. All the limitations on what I could say, on what I could do. I wasn't the heir so I didn't see why I should have to follow them.'

Inara opened her mouth, but he held up a hand, silencing her. She might as well know everything now.

'My father told me I had to come on the trip, that I wasn't allowed to say no. But I was angry with him, so I made Caspian go in my stead. My brother wouldn't have been on that helicopter if it hadn't been for me. In fact, there would have been no trip at all if it hadn't been for me and my terrible behaviour. My entire family would still be alive.'

Her mouth had gone so soft, her eyes liquid. 'Cassius…'

'So you can call me a martyr all you like,' he went on, as if she hadn't spoken. 'But my father and my brother left me a legacy, and I will continue that legacy, to the best of my ability, for as long as I can. I will be the king my brother never got a chance to be and I will continue to do that until the day I die. It will be my memorial to them.'

Her expression twisted and she reached out a hand to him, but he was done. He'd got rid of his secret, he'd told her, and now that was over he had a job to do.

'I will see you tonight, little one.' He found a thread of his usual calm and held on tightly to it. 'In the meantime, I have a job to do.'

And, ignoring her hand, he turned on his heel and went out.

CHAPTER NINE

INARA SAT IN one of the formal sitting rooms in the palace, her head aching. One of the palace historians had been giving her a lecture on the history of the de Leon royal family for the past couple of hours but she had a horrible feeling that, no matter how hard she tried, she was going to remember precisely none of it.

Not that she hadn't tried. She really had because, after Cassius had told her about his family and the legacy he was trying to carry on, she'd decided she had to make this work. Because, like it or not, she was part of that legacy. And she couldn't let her part be a chaotic queen smashing glasses, forgetting names and dashing out of the palace when things went wrong.

That morning, when she'd found him in his study, she'd automatically treated him the way she had when he'd used to visit her, putting a casual hand on his back and wanting to know what he was doing. But he'd stiffened and then gone distant, shrugging her hand away. Becoming the King.

Perhaps she shouldn't have got angry, but the way he'd shrugged off her touch, after being so hungry for it the night before, had hurt. He was a different man when he was the King, and she didn't like it. And, what was more, she was tired of it.

She shouldn't have called him a martyr, though; that had been far too blunt. Especially given what he'd told her about his brother, about his parents. About how he was to blame for it. She'd wanted to know more, to talk to him about it, but he'd turned and walked out before she could.

She'd thought he might say more that night, when she'd been summoned to his rooms, but conversation clearly had not been on his mind. She'd stepped into his bedroom to find him pacing before the fire and she'd barely greeted him before he'd crossed the room, taken her in his arms and then taken her to bed.

And he'd kept her there all night.

That had set the pattern for the past week. Her days were full of 'queen training', as she liked to think of it, while her nights were full of him and 'wife training'. The wife training she liked. She took to those lessons enthusiastically, and she never forgot them either, because learning how to please him pleased her too.

But he didn't talk more about his family or about himself and, even though he'd check in with her during whatever lesson she was having at the time, the only conversation they had was about how she was getting on and whether she was finding it difficult. He was always pleasant and calm and, though he was less condescending, he was no less distant.

That part she didn't like. That part she wanted to change. It wasn't the King she wanted, it was the man he was when he was with her in the depths of the night, warm and vital and hungry. Except she didn't know how to reach that man.

Inara bent over her notepad, hoping the historian wouldn't see as she closed her eyes and rubbed at her temples, trying to get rid of the headache.

'The Queen is tired,' a deep voice said. 'I think that's enough for one day.'

Inara looked up sharply.

Cassius stood in the doorway, dressed in an immaculate dark suit, white shirt and a tie the same smoky gold as his eyes. He glanced briefly at her, his expression impenetrable, then strode over to the historian and had a brief murmured conversation before the man nodded and went out, leaving Inara and Cassius alone.

'I'm all right,' Inara said, annoyed by her headache and the peremptory way Cassius had dismissed the man. 'I was just tired.'

Cassius came over to the uncomfortable couch she was sitting on, giving her a critical once-over. 'You're not all right. You're wearing those contacts again and I can see the circles under your eyes.'

'And who's fault is that?' she said crossly. 'And as for the contacts—'

'They're not needed,' he finished for her, still infuriatingly calm. 'I told you that you could wear your glasses. Why aren't you?'

'I was trying to get used to the contacts.' She rubbed at her eyes. 'Give me a few days and it'll get better.'

'Inara.'

'What?' She glared at him.

He stared back, his gaze very direct. 'I've been talking with people and they all say the same thing. That you have difficulty concentrating, that you don't retain the information you're given and that you're finding it difficult.'

Anger wound through her, along with a certain defensiveness. She'd hoped to have improved since last week, especially as she was now trying even harder, and him finding out that she hadn't was galling.

'I'm trying,' she said flatly. 'But all this protocol and etiquette and other royal stuff...' She stared down at the notepad on which she'd written no notes whatsoever, flashing back to the endless social etiquette drills her mother had put her through. 'Or maybe it's just me.'

There was a moment's silence and then, unexpectedly, Cassius said, 'It's not just you.'

She glanced up at him, surprised. 'Oh?'

'It was...difficult for me too.'

His expression gave nothing away, and yet she heard something almost reluctant in his voice, as if he hadn't meant to say it.

Interesting. That was not what she'd thought he'd say. A memory came back to her, of him in his study and how he'd mentioned that he'd hated all the rules and restrictions placed on him. Was that part of it?

'Why?' she asked, curious now. 'I'd have

thought it would have been easy for you, when you were brought up with all of this.'

'Just because I was brought up with it, doesn't mean it was easy.' He sat down beside her, sadly not close enough to touch; during the day it was obvious he preferred some separation between them, which she found annoying, yet she wasn't quite brave enough to push it. Not yet.

'My father always insisted on stillness and absolute attention,' he went on. 'He said it was rude to fidget and to look bored, and that one of the first rules of being a good ruler was to be patient and attentive to whomever was speaking.'

Cassius let out a breath. 'But I could never sit still or concentrate, and I found all the protocol and royal etiquette we had to learn boring. Caspian never had a problem with it, only me.' He glanced at her, an unexpected glint in his eyes. 'I used to escape into the gardens to hide with the head gardener. He'd tell me all about the plants he was putting in the ground, and how they grew and what they needed, and I found that far more interesting.'

Inara didn't want to move. She didn't even want to breathe. He wasn't the King now. She could tell. He was Cassius, sitting beside her, talking to her the way he used to. She wasn't sure what had prompted the change, but one thing she did know: she wanted to keep him like this for as long as possible.

'So is that why you have all those plants in your study?' She kept the question neutral. 'You said they helped your mind settle.'

'Yes, they do. I still remember telling my father that I wanted to be a gardener, not a prince.' There was a note of dry humour in his voice. 'He wasn't impressed.'

Inara smiled, thinking of Cassius as a little boy, digging earnestly in the dirt. 'I'd imagine not.'

'You need something similar, I think.' There was a shrewd look in his eyes. 'And you already have it, don't you? Numbers are your escape.'

A little jolt went through her. She hadn't expected him to know what mathematics meant to her, let alone to have thought about it. They'd discussed it, of course, but she just hadn't expected him to remember.

'Yes,' she said, her cheeks heating with a ridiculous blush. 'I suppose they are. Numbers feel easier than dealing with people.'

'Easier than etiquette and protocol, yes?'

She nodded. 'And talking to people and all that…social stuff.'

'Yes, I remember. You found that difficult.'

A warm feeling blossomed in her heart. He'd remembered their conversations, when she'd chattered artlessly about how painful her upbringing had been.

'It still is, to be honest.' Inara picked up her pen and fiddled with it. 'And Mama didn't help. She watched everything I did and always had a criticism. It was always, "Stand up straight, Inara. Smile. Be more graceful. If you can't be beautiful, then for God's sake at least be interesting."' She stopped, her throat tight and, though she could feel Cassius's gaze on her, she didn't want to look at him. She couldn't bear the thought of him measuring her against the same impossible standard her mother had once used.

Firstly, would he really do that? And secondly, do you care?

Perhaps he wouldn't. His standards for himself were high, but he didn't put those onto other people. And, as for whether she cared or not, sadly, she did.

Be brave. You're stronger than that.

It was true. She brought a king to his knees

every night. Surely she could look that same king in the eye during the day, unafraid of his judgment?

Inara lifted her chin and looked at him. 'I couldn't do any of those things. I couldn't stand up straight or smile or be graceful. I couldn't be beautiful, and I could certainly never be interesting. That's why they lost patience with me. That's why they gave me to Stefano Castelli.'

Cassius's gaze was steady and direct, a familiar heat burning in it. 'If you're expecting me to agree with your mother's opinions, then you're going to be disappointed,' he said levelly. 'Because I'm glad you couldn't do all those things. I'm glad you failed. And I'm glad that you were given to Stefano Castelli, because otherwise you wouldn't have come to my limo that night. And you wouldn't now be my wife.'

The warmth in her chest blossomed further.

'Not that I would call any of that a failure,' he went on. 'I've always thought you were interesting, and indeed beautiful, though I shouldn't have thought that when you were sixteen.' He paused, holding her gaze. 'You're even more beautiful now.'

Her eyes prickled, the warmth flowing through

her. How strange that being told such lovely things should make her feel like crying.

She wanted to say something—maybe that he was wrong, that only at night in his arms she felt it might be true—but her voice had somehow become stuck in her throat.

Not that she needed to speak, because he continued, 'I've been going about this wrong. I've been forcing you into all the same things as your mother.'

'You're not forcing me,' she managed thickly. 'I'm doing all of this because I want to.'

'Why?'

It was on the tip of her tongue to tell him that he hadn't exactly given her a choice, but then that wasn't quite true, was it? She could have said no. She wasn't sixteen any more, with all her choices made by her parents. She was a grown woman and her choices were her own, and being here in this palace, with him, was a choice she'd made.

Inara swallowed and gave him the truth. 'Why do you think? Because it's important to you, and what's important to you is important to me.'

He said nothing. He just stared at her, his expression utterly impenetrable.

'You said your reign was your memorial to your family, your legacy,' Inara went on, needing to say it. 'And I don't want to be the weak link in that legacy. I want you to have a queen you can be proud of, because let's face it… You didn't exactly choose me. You got stuck with me.'

Some intense emotion flickered over his face, but it was gone before she could name it. He looked away, then abruptly pushed himself off the couch and walked over to one of the long windows that looked out over the formal gardens. He stood there tensely a moment, then said, 'That's true. I didn't choose you. But I wouldn't say I was "stuck" with you.' He turned around, his gaze suddenly fierce. 'You're not a weak link either. I'm already proud of you.'

The warmth in her chest felt like the first touch of sun after a long, cold winter.

'But I haven't done anything except forget people's names, smash glasses and run away.'

'You've done something.' His gaze intensified. 'You're here. You did your best to learn and, even when it doesn't quite work, you're still here and you're still trying. That's tenacity,

Inara. And resilience and courage. And queens need all of those things.'

The sun rose higher inside her, warming her straight through, thawing something that had been frozen in the centre of her soul.

He meant it. He *was* proud of what she was doing.

She opened her mouth to thank him, but then he said suddenly, 'This protocol and etiquette you're learning is nonsense. And we're wasting your talents. Numbers are your strength and Aveiras can benefit from it.' He gave her a narrow look then strode back over to the couch again. 'I should be introducing you to our finance minister and you and he can talk economics.'

Inara hadn't done much with economics but it couldn't be worse than what she was doing now. 'I thought you needed someone to do all the social engagements and be gracious and talk to people.'

'Yes, but I can do that. The people stuff is my strength.' He gave her a sudden brief smile, like a shaft of sunlight glinting through cloud. 'This is a partnership. We share the load.'

Her heart throbbed in her chest and impulsively she reached out to him. 'You really mean that?'

He glanced down at her hand then took it in his, threading his fingers through hers. Warmth travelled up her arm and into her heart, making a home for itself. 'Yes, I mean that.' He looked at her. 'You have many skills, Inara. We were just focusing on the wrong ones.'

Her heart warmed. Everything inside her warmed.

'Maybe that's what happened with you too,' she said unthinkingly. 'Your father should have concentrated on the things you did well, not the things you didn't.'

He stilled, like a man carved from stone. 'And what things do I do well?' The words were so determinedly neutral that she could tell this was important to him. Strange. She hadn't thought her opinion would matter too much to him.

'Well, you *are* good with people. And you're very protective. You notice things. You're observant. And you're very patient. You care about your subjects and your country, all the people you're responsible for. Their well-being matters to you.' She took a breath and smiled. 'You have serious green fingers. You're also extremely good at kissing—which not many people know about you, I don't think. Or at least, they'd better not.' Another pause. 'You also have a wicked sense of humour and when you smile the whole world stops.'

He stared at her, and it seemed as if he might say something, but he didn't.

Instead, after a moment, he gently removed his fingers from hers and walked away without a word. Leaving Inara sitting there with the warmth of his touch lingering on her skin, while a cold thread wound through the warmth in her heart.

Cassius dealt with a few last pressing issues then turned his attention to the grand ball he was in the process of organising in order to formally introduce and welcome Inara as Queen. This one was to be even more formal than the one he'd held a couple of weeks earlier, as this one would not only include heads of state from other countries, but an appearance on the balcony of the palace where the people could welcome her.

The balcony appearance was a grand tradition in Aveiras; it had to be done and possibly was both the easiest and the hardest of the formal occasions. Easy because it required nothing but standing there and waving, hard because the Aveiran people weren't shy when it came to voicing their displeasure if they didn't like something.

And Cassius wanted them to like Inara. He wanted them to welcome her. She wasn't the kind of queen his mother had been. She was… different. But over the past week he'd begun to think that different might be a good thing. Since he'd stopped the etiquette and protocol lessons, and all the other nonsense, replacing it instead with meetings with his finance ministry and the various economic branches of his parliament, she'd blossomed.

Money and numbers bored him to tears, but not her. She'd taken to it like a duck to water, involving herself in all aspects of Aveiras's economy, using her clear, logical brain to work on some of the country's thorny financial difficulties, and then pointing out several new ways they could fill the treasury. She had a gift not only for numbers, but for money and the financial markets, which would benefit Aveiras considerably.

He'd continued to oversee her progress, and

for the past week the only feedback he'd had about her was glowing praise of what a brilliant thinker she was, how perceptive she was when it came to economics and how she had the potential to revolutionise the country's fiscal policy.

His finance ministers loved her, and he knew he shouldn't take pride in seeing her walk by him, sometimes deep in conversation with a small group of ministers and advisors, but he did. Especially when it was clear her stylists hadn't caught her in time and she was dressed in one of her floaty dresses with her hair loose over her shoulders.

Sometimes he'd even stand in the corridor, waiting to see if she'd notice him as she swept by, but most of the time she didn't. And neither did his ministers. It amused him that they'd be so deep in conversation they didn't even notice their king. However, he was less than amused when Inara didn't notice him. Which was new. Most of the time he found the constant attention from people tiring, but apparently that didn't extend to her.

Cassius frowned as he went over the plans for the ball, not seeing them as his mind drifted once more to his wife. His pretty little fairy of a wife who couldn't care less about clothes or balls or appearances, who could balance a budget in seconds and who was as hungry for him as he was for her when she came to him every night.

He'd told her a week ago, when he'd found her red-eyed and miserable in one of the formal sitting rooms, that they were a match, and even though he hadn't thought so initially, he was beginning to see the truth of that now.

When he'd looked at her that day, the feedback about her from his consultants filling his head, he'd seen himself all those years ago trying to sit through endless lessons about things that hadn't interested him, cudgelling his reluctant brain into retaining dates and names and arcane, pointless protocol. Trying and always failing.

At the time he'd thought there was something wrong with him, as he'd never had any issues concentrating or remembering things when it came to scientific plant names and what specific conditions each plant needed to grow. But there hadn't been anything wrong with him.

Because look at him now, doing everything his father had, everything Caspian had, and doing it successfully. He'd overcome his failings, his flaws, but he wouldn't put Inara through the same mill by insisting. Because, if there was one thing he'd learned during the last three years, it was that people performed better when you focused on and utilised their strengths, rather than fixing their failings. If people were happy and enjoying themselves, then the resulting confidence boost tended to minimise those failings anyway.

And you? What about you?

He was irrelevant. He was the King and his enjoyment, his happiness, didn't matter.

Not that you deserve any.

Cassius abruptly pushed away the plans he'd been staring at. This train of thought was pointless. Perhaps some time in the garden was needed to settle himself. He hadn't yet told Inara about the ball, which he should have done, but she'd seemed happy and much more settled recently and he didn't want to upset her.

Since when have her feelings become important to you? If yours aren't relevant, then hers aren't either.

Cassius shoved his chair back and got to his feet, trying to ignore that thought. Because it was wrong. Of course her feelings mattered, as did everyone's. The King's didn't because he was the leader, the figurehead. He was the example everyone looked to, the example everyone followed. You couldn't have feelings as a king. You couldn't be a person, not in the same way as everyone else. Inara had accused him of being a martyr, but she was wrong. He hadn't nailed himself to a cross when he'd taken his crown. He'd taken it willingly. And he was at peace with his role.

So at peace you walked out of a ball you should have remained at to follow a woman because you were angry. And then you took her to bed because you wanted her. And then you stopped important, vital protocol lessons to make her happy. And now you can't concentrate on the ball you're supposed to be organising because all you can think about is her...

Cassius gritted his teeth as he strode down the echoing marble hallways of the palace, not wanting to acknowledge the truth of all of that, yet not able to ignore it either. Because it *was* true. There had been minimal fallout from the ball, but only because of the stellar work of his PR team.

And, with another formal ball coming up, halting Inara's protocol lessons had possibly been a mistake. He should insist she continue with them. He should get stricter with her, not relax the rules. Necessity had finally made all his father's lessons stick; perhaps he should try the same tactics with her.

No, this isn't about her. It's about you. You taking her to bed every night. You indulging your own appetites, your weaknesses, your flaws...

Tension gripped him as he approached his private apartments, giving a curt nod to his guards as they opened the doors for him and he stepped through. He'd thought he could keep what happened at night in his bed separate from his duties during the day, that he could keep the man separate from the King, but it was becoming very clear that was impossible. Yet he'd already tried denying himself, and that hadn't worked, so what else could he do?

Perhaps it was his need to hold her after they'd made love that was the issue. His need to drown in her scent and listen to the sound of her breathing. The strange desperation he had to get closer, even when he knew what he should do was keep his distance. He could allow himself a physical release, but anything more, anything emotional, was...wrong.

It was his emotions that had led him astray, after all, his frustration as child and then his impatience with the restrictions imposed on him as a young man. His anger at his father's continual disapproval.

Perhaps he needed to limit Inara's visits. Perhaps he needed to turn her away or not send for her. At least for a little while, or maybe just not every night, enough to remind himself that his own desires were not paramount. And maybe that would help him be stricter with her during the day. He couldn't compromise the legacy he was trying to build. Not again.

He came to the door of his study, noting with displeasure that it was open, which meant that one of the cleaning staff hadn't closed it properly. Annoying. He kept the room at a specific temperature optimal for his plants, as several didn't like the cool of the rest of the palace, which meant he preferred to keep the doors closed.

Irritated, he made a mental note to remind staff to always close the door, then he stepped inside himself, closing it firmly behind him.

Only to discover that the room wasn't empty.

Inara sat in one of the blue velvet arm chairs. She had a stack of papers on her knees, some of them overflowing onto the floor, and various pens scattered on the cushions next to her. On a small side table beside the arm chair stood three teacups, all with different liquids in them; the small orchid he kept there had been shoved unceremoniously to one side.

Today she wore a pencil skirt and a plain white blouse, but the pencil skirt was creased, the blouse crumpled and coming unbuttoned. Her hair was in what had probably once been a neat chignon, but was now half-coming down, silvery wisps haloing her face and one long lock draping over her shoulder. A pair of high-heeled pumps was scattered on the carpet in front of the arm chair, as if she'd just kicked them off and left them where they lay.

She should have looked like a disaster, the very antithesis of a queen, and yet... All he could think about was what one of his financial team had told him the day before, raving about how approachable the Queen was, how accessible. Making it obvious that Cassius's parents suffered in comparison.

It had shocked him. His father had always been held up as the ideal, and Caspian had followed in his footsteps. But it could never be said that Cassius's father had been either accessible or approachable. *Be respectful*, his father had always said, *but maintain your distance*. Allowing people to get too familiar undermined your authority, and above all a king had to maintain his authority.

People had respected his father, yet he hadn't been an easy man to get to know. He had been reserved, never demonstrative. He had been gracious and perfectly pleasant to his subjects, but distant, remaining a cipher, an enigma, even to his sons.

There was nothing enigmatic about Inara. She sat in his study, in his armchair, with her shoes off, papers everywhere, half-drunk cups of tea crowding out his plant, her hair coming down. And yet… She wasn't distant. She wasn't chilly. She was approachable. Accessible.

She was human.

His heart clenched tightly for no apparent reason. And then she looked up from her papers, seeing him, her beautiful mouth curving in a smile like the sun rising. And the tightness in his heart constricted further, his whole body tensing in a kind of shock. As if her smile was something that hurt him.

'Oh, hi,' she said. 'I hope you don't mind. I couldn't concentrate in the Queen's office, so I thought I'd come in here. It's such a relaxing space...' She trailed off. Whatever expression was on his face, it couldn't be anything good, as her smile faded. 'I'm sorry,' she went on quickly. 'I'll go. It was probably a bit forward of me to—'

'Stay.' His voice came out far rougher than he'd intended. 'I'll come back later.'

But Inara's brow creased. 'I don't want to intrude on your space. I'll stay very quiet, I promise. I always do when I'm working.'

Part of him wanted to leave, to put some distance between her and the tight feeling in his chest, but he also didn't want to let that feeling win.

'All right,' he allowed. 'But stay quiet.'

She nodded, giving him another quick smile then returning her attention to her stack of papers.

Cassius moved over to begin his inventory of the bonsai and the other plants. And it was with some surprise that he found himself not quite forgetting she was there, but finding her presence...restful. It was strange, given her general level of untidiness, but she was silent while she worked, the only sound the faint rustling of paper and the scratching of her pen.

A companionable silence settled over the room and some time passed...he wasn't sure how long. The tight feeling in his chest had faded, the snide voice in his head quietening. He watered the last of his plants and then turned, moving over to the arm chair opposite hers and sitting in it.

She didn't look up, still furiously writing something. Not wanting to interrupt, he relaxed, letting the silence and peace of the room seep into him. After a moment, Inara looked up from her work and gave him another of those heart-breakingly beautiful smiles.

'You like working with a pen and paper?' he asked, idly curious. 'Not a computer?'

'No. Writing it down myself helps me feel more...connected to whatever problem I'm working on. Which probably sounds weird.'

'No weirder than a king who likes pottering with his houseplants.'

She laughed, the sound delighting him, as it

had been a long time since he'd made a woman laugh.

'It's clearly good for you, though.' She tilted her head, giving him a speculative look. Then she put aside her papers and pen, got out of her chair and came over to him.

He stayed where he was, curious to see what she intended. Probably a mistake, given his earlier thoughts on the subject, but he found he couldn't bring himself to move.

He liked her being here. He liked being in the same room, both of them doing separate things, yet together. It made him realise that he hadn't had the company of another person in quite this way for three years… No, longer. In fact, had he ever had this quiet, companionable feeling with another person? Even back when he'd been a prince, the company he'd kept had been of the loud, drunken variety, or soft, welcoming and female. And working quietly had been the last thing on his mind.

Inara reached for his tie and loosened it.

'What are you doing, little one?'

'Helping you relax.' She pulled the tie away from his neck, bending over him to undo the buttons on his shirt.

He should stop her, he really should, because her scent was surrounding him, along with the warmth of her body, and it made him think of the previous night when he'd had her beneath him, panting in his ear…

'I'm not sure taking my tie off will help me relax.' He looked up at her. 'In fact, I can safely say that relaxed is the last thing I feel with your hands on me.'

She wrinkled her nose, going the most adorable shade of pink as she fussed with his buttons. 'I'm not talking about *that*. You're always so…uptight. You could stand to be a little… looser.'

He wanted to pull her down into his lap, cover that gorgeous mouth with his own, and it was difficult to remember why that was a bad idea. Certainly, his brain had told him something of the sort earlier, but with her bending over him, so pretty and warm and human, he couldn't seem to remember why that was such a bad idea. He couldn't seem to remember why any of the things he'd been telling himself about following his father's example and leaving a legacy was such a good thing. Not when she was here.

You know it's not about leaving a legacy. Or even following an example. You're punishing yourself, because it's what you deserve.

Inara's fingers were warm at his throat, brushing his skin as she pulled open the buttons of his shirt, but he felt suddenly cold, as if all the blood in his veins were icing over. He'd reached up to brush her hands away before he could stop himself.

Instantly Inara straightened, her expressive features tightening. 'I'm sorry, I didn't mean…'

'It's fine.' He pushed himself out of the chair, all his good feelings draining away.

No, this had been a mistake. He should be back in his office, preparing for this ball, not here in his study, indulging himself.

Indulging himself. That had always been his problem.

'It's not fine,' Inara said. 'What did I do?' She was standing in front of him, blocking his path to the door, her grey eyes full of concern.

'Nothing,' he said curtly. 'Move, please, Inara. I have to get back to work.'

Something flickered in her gaze, that spark of challenge, the sign of a will that was becoming more and more formidable.

'I did do something.' She stayed exactly where she was. 'You were fine until I undid your tie.'

'Because it reminded me that now isn't the time to relax,' he snapped. 'It's the middle of the day and I should—'

'If it was only that, you wouldn't be so angry. And you're angry, Cassius, I can see it in your eyes.'

He took a breath, fighting down the heat gathering inside him. 'It's nothing you did,' he forced out calmly. 'Please, Inara, I have to—'

'Why?' There was something fierce in her gaze now, a silver flame, burning brightly. 'You're angry at something. Is it me? Because this is the second time you've walked away from me without a word.'

He tried to find the calmness inside him, the patience he needed to control his emotions.

'I'm not angry,' he said, knowing even as he said it that it was a lie. Because he could feel that heat inside him growing ever hotter, burning more furiously, and all the denying in the world wasn't going to make it go away.

Inara's mouth softened, the crease between her brows deepening. 'You'd forgotten, hadn't you?

You'd forgotten for a moment that you were a king and something made you remember.'

She was right. He wasn't sure how she knew, how she could see that in him, but it was true.

Before he could say a word, she stepped forward, raising a hand to his cheek, her palm warm against his skin. 'It's okay, Cassius. You can have a few moments of forgetfulness. Surely that's allowed?'

His hand came up before he could stop it, circling her wrist and pulling that comforting palm away. 'No,' he said woodenly. 'It isn't allowed. I can't forget, Inara. I can't ever forget. Self-indulgence and selfishness got my family killed and it will taint my reign if I let it. Remembering what happened and who I was is the only way I can make sure that my father's legacy remains intact.'

'I understand why that's important to you. But your father is gone… And so is your brother. *You* are the King. So shouldn't your reign be *your* legacy rather than theirs?'

Something echoed inside him, like a bell tolling, but he ignored it, the flames of his deep, formless anger burning too high.

'Yes, why not?' He released her wrist, bitterness tingeing the words. 'A legacy of parties and drunkenness and sex. Of a petty prince indulging his own petulant resentment. A legacy of selfishness. Yes, that's exactly what Aveiras needs, a king who puts his own emotions before the needs of his subjects.'

She stared at him as if he were a stranger. 'Is that really how you see yourself? How you saw yourself back then?'

'It's not how I see myself,' he spat. 'It's how I *was*.'

Her chin came up, the silver flame flickering in her eyes, as if she was preparing to challenge him. 'No, that's *not* what you were. What you were was a man who helped a lost and desperate teenager. Who protected her. Who visited her and showed an interest in her that no one ever had. A man who discussed things with her, laughed with her, made her feel good about herself for the first time in her life. A man who, when his family died, stepped up and took responsibility even though he didn't need to.'

The ferocity in her gaze gripped him, held him still. 'That's the kind of man you were, Cassius. Yes, you had failings, didn't we all? But punishing yourself for yours isn't going to give you the legacy you're trying to build. It'll only end up tearing you apart.'

Her words felt like arrows, striking him in unprotected parts of his body, causing pain wherever they landed.

'You're wrong.' His voice was finally stripped of all emotion. 'I was never that man. That man was a lie.'

Her gaze flickered then, as if the flame in it had finally burned out. 'Fine,' she said. 'Tell me I'm wrong. Tell me I was too young, too innocent. That I didn't know my own feelings. But nothing will change the way I saw you then, Cassius, and nothing is going to change the way I feel now. You're still that man underneath. I know you are. And, whether you like it or not, that man was a good person.'

She took a little breath. 'I…loved that man.'

It felt as though she'd struck him with a punch direct to the gut, stealing all his air.

'What?' His voice echoed strangely in his head.

She just looked at him, the truth laid bare in her face, in her eyes. A truth that had probably been there all this time. He'd just never seen it.

You never wanted to see it, either.

She stared at him a second longer, then lifted her hand once more and touched his cheek briefly.

Then she turned and, not stopping even to grab her shoes, went out of the room. This time leaving him to be the one who was alone.

CHAPTER TEN

INARA FOUND IT difficult to work the rest of the day. It was even harder when Cassius didn't send for her that night, leaving her to pace about the Queen's cold and echoing apartments by herself.

It wasn't any mystery why he didn't send for her, though. She'd confronted him, pushed him. Then she'd thrown that confession at him and he'd looked...stunned. As if she'd slapped him or hit him over the head.

Perhaps she shouldn't have said it. Then again, she didn't regret telling him, because she hadn't been able to stand the self-loathing in his voice. He hated the prince he'd once been and she could understand it. He believed he'd sent his entire family to their deaths, and it was obvious he was trying to put as much distance between himself and that person as he could. She understood. She really did.

But she'd fallen in love with that man and she loved him still. And she hated the way he viewed himself. She didn't see someone who'd killed his family. She saw a warm, empathetic prince who'd protected her, talked to her, been interested in her. Who'd made her feel good about herself for the first time in her life.

Yes, he had his failings. He was angry, and even back then she'd been able to see that anger. It had been evident in the edge to his voice whenever he spoke about his father, and it had been clear that he was unhappy. She'd often wished she knew why, but she hadn't been brave enough to ask, and he'd never said.

But she thought she knew now. It had something to do with what he'd told her that day in the sitting room, about how he'd never been able to sit through those lessons in royal etiquette. How he'd had to escape into the gardens and how his parents had been so disapproving of him.

She ached for that little boy. She wanted to gather him into her arms and hold him, tell him it was okay to be the way he was. That he had his strengths, and they were just different from his brother's and his father's, just as hers were different. That he was just as worthy, just as admirable, as they were.

But she suspected the helicopter crash had only turned the scratches his family had inflicted into mortal wounds.

He couldn't accept himself as he was, and she knew deep in her heart that if he continued trying to be the king his father had wanted, the king his brother should have been, then it would eventually tear him apart. And as his queen she'd have to stand by and watch him disintegrate, unable to do anything for him. Unable to help.

She *hated* the thought of it.

Days went by and the only communication she had from him was notification of the formal ball that would take place to introduce her to the nation. She was in a meeting with one of her favourite financial ministers when she heard, and for a second she just looked at the note that had been passed to her, her heart beating very fast.

But not because she was afraid, though a couple of weeks ago this would have been her worst nightmare. Now, it gave her an idea. She kept that idea in her head the whole day, letting it sit there, shining brightly, and only once she was alone in the Queen's apartments did she examine it closely from all angles.

If she wanted to save her king, there was only

one thing she could do. She had to show him there was a different way. A better way. That he didn't need to base his entire life on examples that trapped him, that hurt him, that denied who he was deep down. That instead he should be true to himself, trust that he could be the king he was meant to be, not the king he thought he *should* be.

It might not work, but it was all she could think of. Especially given his tendency to distance her whenever she got too close. That last time she'd been the one to walk away, but only because she'd known that if she stayed the rest of what was in her heart would come tumbling out. How it wasn't only the Prince she cared about, but the King as well. They were both part of the man. And it was the man she loved, every difficult, sharp and complicated part of him.

But she couldn't tell him that. He'd only distance her even more.

He stayed away the entire week, closing himself off, and she let him. She didn't want to give away any part of what she intended for the upcoming ball, because she was certain that if he knew he'd try and stop her.

More lessons in protocol appeared on her

schedule, and this time at the King's insistence. She didn't protest. She sat through them, giving all the appearance of listening avidly while her mind took note of all the things she *wasn't* going to do.

Because he was wrong. And his father had been wrong too. It wasn't protocol and etiquette that made a good king, it was connecting with people. And that wasn't something she'd thought of two weeks ago and, even though he didn't realise it, it was Cassius who'd showed her that.

He'd told her that Aveiras should use her strengths and, since being involved with Aveiras's finances, which she'd discovered she loved, she'd realised how powerful that was. That it wasn't people as a whole she had difficulty interacting with—she had no problem talking to the ministers and staff in the finance ministry—just some people.

And that was okay. Not remembering names was okay. It was the connection that mattered, being interested in someone and demonstrating that. She still needed practice in that area, but for Cassius it was instinctive.

If only he could see that.

* * *

The week passed far too quickly.

She made no effort to contact him. Sometimes she heard his deep voice echoing in the cold halls of the palace and had to stop herself from running after him. That would undermine the point she wanted to make, so she didn't. Instead, she made sure every report the etiquette people took back to him was glowing—that the Queen was making progress and they were happy with her efforts.

A schedule of events, seating plans, names and potted histories of VIPs arrived. She was advised who to talk to, whose hand to shake, who to merely nod at and who actively not to show favour to. Times were given and she was told very sternly that they must be adhered to. She nodded and smiled and forgot everything. Purposely.

A gown arrived, formal and decidedly neutral, stiff with embroidery. She allowed herself to be fitted for it without complaint, while in secret she talked to one of the royal dressmaker's assistants. She didn't want the King to know what she was planning, so everything had to be kept hidden.

The night of the ball soon arrived and Inara was led away hours beforehand to be scrubbed and plucked and primped to within an inch of her life, zipped up into the armour of a dress, painful contacts in her eyes. Her hair was smooth, sleek and shining, coiled up into intricate twists on her head, held in place by diamond pins. Careful contouring of her face was done, with a metric ton of make-up designed to look as if she was wearing no make-up at all.

And, last of all, the crown of Aveiras—thick and ancient gold set with antique diamonds, and brilliantly blue sapphires to represent the sea. It was heavy and made her head hurt, and she could only think of poor Cassius and the crown he had to wear, which was even thicker and heavier.

She would free him from that if she could.

With an hour to go, she dismissed her aides and attendants. She wasn't used to giving orders, and had secretly worried that they wouldn't obey her, but when she added that she needed some time to go through the schedules by herself they all agreed.

As soon as the door closed behind them, Inara sprang into action.

It didn't take long. Everything she needed had been delivered to her apartments earlier that day, so it was all to hand. She was ready in half an hour, which was half an hour before the King and Queen were to appear at the ball.

Perfect timing.

Inara didn't wait to be summoned. Didn't wait to call her attendants back. She simply strode along the cold, marble hallways of the palace, past the judgmental eyes of the de Leon rulers.

She ignored them.

The double doors of the ballroom were closed, the guards stationed outside staring at her in some surprise as she approached. She gestured at them and, after a glance at each other, they pulled the doors open for her.

Inara didn't hesitate. She strode through into the glittering light of the ballroom, surrounded by the buzz of conversation and music, the loud noise of hundreds of people all gathered in one place.

The usher by the stairs looked at her in consternation, but she only smiled. 'I know,' she said. 'I'm early. Announce me anyway.'

The usher glanced behind her, as if he hoped to see the King, or anyone who might countenance this complete break with tradition, but there was only Inara. And she was the Queen.

He took a breath, then nodded and turned to the crowded ballroom.

'Her Royal Majesty, Queen Inara of Aveiras,' he announced loudly.

Everyone stopped talking and turned in her direction.

Inara braced herself, then started down the stairs.

'Your Majesty, the Queen is already there.'

Cassius, in the middle of inspecting the crown he wore for official occasions, looked up. 'What? What you do you mean, she's already there?'

The aide looked apologetic. 'I mean, Her Majesty arrived at the ball twenty minutes ago.'

Shock and anger twisted in Cassius's stomach.

He and Inara were supposed to enter the ballroom together, the way they had the week before, properly announced and properly greeted. She should know that; he'd sent her the schedule days ago. Had she forgotten? She'd had difficulty with the schedules and protocols and etiquette…he knew that. But his people had assured him that the Queen had been attending their sessions and knew exactly what was expected of her.

He hadn't monitored her personally. He'd simply let her know that these things would be required and had expected her to comply.

It was the only way. He couldn't allow what she'd told him that day in his study to matter. He couldn't allow it to affect him. She'd said she loved the man he'd once been and the truth of it had been there in her eyes.

But she'd been blind. That was her problem. How could she love a man that selfish, that self-centred? That flawed? A man so consumed with his own petty annoyances and ridiculous grievances that he hadn't seen the damage he was causing.

That's not the way she sees you and she told you that.

No. She'd told him that he'd made her feel good about herself, made her laugh. Protected her.

Punishing yourself...isn't going to give you the legacy you're trying to build. It'll only end up tearing you apart.

He could still hear those words in his head, and they made even less sense now than they had at the time. He wasn't punishing himself. He was simply doing what needed to be done.

Regardless, he couldn't afford to think about this now. Inara was somehow going off script and he needed to get her back onto it. This was an important ball and she had to get things right if she wanted to be accepted by the people of Aveiras.

'I'll be there directly,' he said in curt tones, dismissing the aide.

He didn't bother with the crown, leaving his rooms and striding straight to the ballroom. The guards spotted him and instantly threw the doors wide.

He went on through then paused at the top of the stairs that led down into the ballroom proper, searching for Inara.

He saw her immediately and all the breath left his body. She wasn't wearing the gown he'd commissioned or the crown of the queens of Aveiras. The gown she wore was simple and un-adorned, a bias-cut slip dress in sapphire-blue satin with a very small, flowing train that flut-tered behind her as she walked. Her hair was in loose silver curls down her back and, instead of the crown, there was a simple circlet of twisted silver strands studded with sapphires. On her feet she wore blue satin slippers, no heels, and on her nose were perched her glasses.

She was surrounded by the finance ministers she knew, plus a couple from other countries, all deep in conversation about something. The people in the ballroom swirled around her, some of them openly disapproving, but more than a few clearly intrigued.

Then, as he watched, Inara broke away from her little coterie and moved over to another group of people—ambassadors from France, from the looks of things. She shook their hands, not bothering to wait for her aide to introduce her, and smiled, exchanging a few words then moving on. She did this a number of times, and then stopped as someone else joined her group and another deep, intense conversation ensued.

His heart felt so tight he couldn't breathe.

She wasn't in the crown or the gown, and she'd arrived early and hadn't waited for him. She was clearly without an aide to introduce her, and as for the schedules…they were apparently long gone.

She wasn't at all the queen he'd wanted or the queen he'd expected. She was…better. She was warm and human and approachable. The gown she wore was simple and yet elegant, flowing around her like water. She looked young and carefree and so heartbreakingly beautiful that the entire world stood still.

The usher saw him standing there transfixed and announced him immediately. It took him a couple of moments to realise that everyone was staring at him and that he hadn't moved because he was too busy staring at Inara.

She turned with everyone else and her lovely face broke into the most incredible smile. Without waiting for him to come to her or for an aide to approach, she marched straight through the crowd and up the stairs. Then she took his hand as if he was merely her lover and not the King, her warm fingers threading through his, and led him down into the crowds.

He knew he should stop her. He should pull her hand from his and insist on the proper protocols, insist that they needed to adhere to the schedule and the timing, because this was a formal event. There were heads of state here and he needed to set an example. But he couldn't bring himself to do it. A part of him was captivated by his lovely wife, and curious to see what she would do and what would happen next.

So he let Inara set the example.

He'd always found royal duties interminable and difficult, something to endure instead of enjoy, but tonight it felt different. It was Inara who led him round instead of his aide, approaching people and asking their names without caring that a queen should already know.

And what was even more surprising was that people didn't seem to mind. She was artless, utterly without guile, completely open and honest. Sometimes awkward, but laughing at herself too, and he could see how that put people at their ease. He had no idea why she'd ever thought she wasn't good at the social stuff, because if anything it was the opposite.

She put something inside him at ease too, a tightly leashed part of himself he never let out. And before he knew what was happening, he was smiling and talking to people as if he was still that prince, the charming one who'd always known what to say to make himself the life of the party.

People responded. He could see it in their faces. And soon he and Inara were surrounded, with more people coming over to talk with them, schedules out of the window, no distance, no formality.

His father would have been appalled.

But as the evening went on Cassius couldn't bring himself to care. Inara's hand was warm inside his, her presence beside him bright and beautiful, and he didn't want to let that hand go. He didn't want her to leave his side. Once or twice he glanced at her to find her looking back, her eyes shining with an emotion that made his heart ache.

Much later, an aide approached them, informing them that they were due to make their appearance on the balcony. As that was one formality they couldn't ignore, he found himself leading Inara from the ballroom and through the corridors to the formal reception room that opened out onto the balcony.

'Why?' he asked quietly as several palace employees began to prepare the room. 'Why did you do all of this?' He didn't elaborate; she'd know what he meant.

Her fingers tightened around his. 'I wanted you to see that you could do something differently. That you didn't have to follow your father's example. That you could do things your way.' She shifted closer, looking up at him, a fierce light in her eyes. 'That you could create a legacy that's yours, that isn't bound by anyone else's protocols or idea of what's right and proper. A legacy that's about you and the kind of king *you* want to be.'

He'd never thought about it in that way before, and it struck him all of a sudden that it was because he'd never really viewed the role of king as his before. It had always been about his father or his brother. A position he'd taken almost as a caretaker of their memory, not something he could put his own stamp on.

But…he could, couldn't he?

Just as Inara had put her own stamp on being a queen.

They're dead because of you, though. Can you really dishonour their legacy like that?

It was true they were dead and, yes, because of him. But was it really such a dishonour to do things differently? To be the kind of king *he* wanted to be, not what his father had been or his brother would have been?

Cassius lifted her hand and pressed his mouth against the back of it, then they were stepping forward to the balcony that overlooked the central city square, the sound of the crowd rolling over them.

He felt Inara tremble beside him, but he lifted her hand and held it out, showing her to his people, and smiled. Cameras everywhere beamed that smile to screens set up around the square and to TVs all over the nation, just as they beamed the approving roar of the crowd.

Adrenalin filled him, a surge of hope he hadn't felt in far too long. Hope that soon turned into something hotter and more joyful, centred on the woman who'd brought him to this point.

His queen. His Inara.

They stepped back from the balcony, and as soon as the doors were closed, and the shutters across the windows pulled tight, Cassius dismissed everyone from the room.

Then he turned to her, glowing and beautiful in her blue gown, and gently but surely pushed her up against the balcony doors.

She didn't protest. Her lovely face was flushed, her eyes still shining, looking at him as if he was the only thing worth looking at in the entire world.

'They loved you,' he said softly. 'I knew they would.'

But this time she didn't smile.

'What about you?' Her voice sounded hoarse. 'Do you love me too?'

CHAPTER ELEVEN

SHE HADN'T MEANT to just come out with it. She hadn't meant to say it at all but, looking out over the crowds, watching them shout for him, cheer for him, gaze at him as if he was the centre of their world, she felt that very same adoration burning like a coal at the centre of her chest.

In that moment, as he'd taken her hand and smiled at the crowd, she hadn't cared if they accepted her or not. She hadn't cared about them at all.

The only thing that mattered to her was him.

And she wanted him.

She wanted to mean something to him too.

Tonight she'd watched him become the kind of king he should be, not bound by his father's legacy or trying to fit his brother's shoes. A less formal, more accessible kind of king. A king who wasn't only respected but who was loved too.

A king she could love. A king she already

loved. It should have been enough to be his wife, to know that she'd helped him be all he could be, the way he'd helped her. To be his queen. To be his lover.

It was more than she'd ever thought she'd have and yet…

It wasn't enough.

And she was scared. While it was clear he was ready to take her to bed again, she wasn't sure how long that would continue. This whole week, he'd shut her out, and he'd done the same the week before. He distanced himself whenever she challenged him, making her feel as if she was walking on egg shells around him, and that felt…precarious.

This situation—their marriage and thus her future—felt precarious. Was this what it would be like between them from now on? Would it be her, loving him from afar, surviving on whatever attention he chose to give her? Never knowing whether she'd say the wrong thing and end up being shut out again?

She'd never had anyone accept her for who she was, not the way he'd accepted her. She'd never had anyone who thought she was beautiful or interesting, or even worth knowing, the way he did. And though that was wonderful, there was still one thing she'd never had, not from anyone.

Love.

Was it so wrong to want that? So wrong to ask for it?

Cassius lifted his head, staring down at her, a hot amber glow burning in his eyes. 'Let's talk about this later.'

'When later?' The words came out before she could stop them. 'Before or after you refuse to speak to me for another week? Or refuse to take me to your bed?'

'Inara, I—'

'It's a simple question, Cassius. Yes or no?' She was trembling all of a sudden, her chest gone tight and sore. 'And I'm guessing that, since you can't answer it, you don't.'

He stared at her for a long moment then took a step back, lifting a hand and shoving it distractedly through his black hair. 'You surprised me. I wasn't expecting you to ask a question like that.'

She swallowed, her heart a piece of broken glass embedded in her chest, jagged and sharp. 'I told you I loved you, Cassius. And then you ignored me for an entire week. You wouldn't even let me come to your bed.'

His hand dropped. 'You told me that you loved the prince.'

'Yes. And I love the King too. I love *you*. I've loved you for years.' There wasn't any point hiding it. He'd told her his secret and now it was her turn to share hers, and there was a kind of freedom in that.

Emotions flickered over his face, gone too fast for her to see what they were, before his features finally settled into the expression she hated so much. The calm one, the condescending one. The mask he used when he wanted to distance people. When he wanted to hide.

'I know I've treated your poorly,' he said levelly. 'I'm sorry. I shouldn't have done that but—'

'Is this what our marriage will be like from now on?' She took a step forward, anger igniting inside her. A cleansing, freeing anger. 'I only get whatever crumbs of attention you give me? Ignored whenever I challenge you, barred from your bed whenever I offend you?'

'No, that's not—'

'Will it be like it was before, Cassius? Will I be banished to the Queen's rooms, like I was banished to the Queen's Estate? Existing only when you choose to recognise my existence?

Wheeled out for state functions or whenever you need a queen on your arm? Summoned only when you need a woman in your bed.'

The calm mask cracked, a fierce glow beginning to burn in his eyes. 'I never banished you. No, I didn't summon you last week, but you never tried to contact me either. You didn't come to my door. You told me you loved the prince I once was and then you walked out.'

It was true. That was exactly what she'd done. 'Because I thought you needed some time to think about it and I didn't want to crowd you. Plus, tonight required a bit of planning, and I didn't want you to know about it. And even if I hadn't been doing all of that, would you have let me in if I'd come to you? Or would you have sent an aide to tell me you were "too busy"?' She took another step towards him, her anger burning hotter. 'And why should I be the one who always has to come to you, anyway? Why should I be the one who has to wait for you to be ready to receive me?'

A muscle flicked in his jaw. 'What is it exactly that you want from me, Inara? You want the freedom to come to my bed whenever it suits you? Is that it?'

'No, you idiot man.' She was now only inches away. 'What I want is a real marriage. I want to be your wife in reality, all the time, not only when it suits you. And I want you to love me the way I love you—because no one ever has, Cassius. Not even my parents.'

His gaze flickered, but there was no softening in his expression. 'You want the truth? You really want an answer? Fine. I don't love you, Inara, and I never will. I'll never love anyone. It's all I can do to carry the weight of the crown, to love my country and my people.'

Inara felt something die a little inside her, the fragile tendril of her hope crushed utterly. Because looking at the hard, set lines of his face and the anger burning in his eyes, it was worse than she'd thought.

Love was a burden to him, an extra weight he didn't need, not with all the expectations he'd heaped on himself already. And why would he expect love to be anything else? After the way he'd been brought up and the standards he'd been measured against by his own family?

Her own had been no different. It was just… her love for him had brought her confidence and freedom. But it was clear that lesson hadn't gone both ways.

You failed. Again.

Inara swallowed past the lump in her throat, trying to find the right words, the right thing, that would help him see. 'Love isn't a weight,' she said thickly. 'It's not a burden to bear. It sets you free. How can you not see that?'

He gave a harsh laugh. 'Free? I loved my parents and my brother, but do I look free to you? Do I look unburdened?'

Tears pricked at her eyes. 'No. You look like a man beating himself to death over something that wasn't his fault in the first place.'

His expression twisted, anger flaring across it. 'Of course it was my fault. I was expected to at least act like a prince of the realm and I couldn't even do that much. I was too selfish, too angry. Too caught up in—'

'You were a boy who'd been measured all his life against standards he could never possibly live up to,' she interrupted, suddenly and completely furious. 'You're just like me. *Exactly* like me. We both had parents who wanted us to be something different, who couldn't accept us for who we were, and I understand how that hurts.

But there comes a point where you have to decide whether to let that be a stick you keep beating yourself with. Or you choose to let it go and accept who you are. Like I did. Like *you* taught me to.'

A light flared in his eyes and for a second she thought she might have got through to him. But then it vanished, forced away beneath that blank mask once again as he took a step back from her, putting distance between them.

'I'm sorry, Inara,' he said, hard and cold. 'But, whether you like it or not, those standards are part of my world now. And I *have* met them. And I'll continue to meet them for the good of my country and my people.'

Her anger drained away just as quickly as it had come, leaving her empty and hollow. It was becoming more and more obvious with every passing moment that there was nothing she could say that would help him.

Nothing she could do.

He was committed to his own punishment and eventually it would crush him.

Her heart broke, that piece of jagged glass splintering, knowing that there was only one choice left for her.

She could stay in this precarious marriage, suffering quietly every day, in the hope that one day his feelings would change, that one day he'd turn around and tell her that he loved her. Or she could leave him, leave this marriage, accepting that change wasn't possible and would never be possible for him.

Everything she'd done since she'd got here had been for him, but she couldn't keep on doing it. She couldn't keep on giving pieces of herself away, getting smaller and smaller, weaker and weaker, every day.

She had to keep something for herself.

'Okay,' Inara said thickly 'If that's the way it has to be, then that's what it has to be. But I'm afraid I'm not going to stay being your wife, Cassius. I can't. I don't want to be banished to the Queen's apartments, or wherever you think I need to be, summoned whenever you need me then forgotten about when you don't. I don't want to be that child bride you visit whenever you're bored. And I can't stay here and watch you tear yourself apart.'

'Inara—'

'Cassius, I want a divorce.'

* * *

He couldn't believe it. His beautiful wife, his lovely queen, the woman who'd showed him that there was a different way, a better way, was asking him for a divorce.

And all because he wouldn't tell her he loved her when she demanded it.

That was love, though, wasn't it? A demand. An expectation. Something that was only given when certain conditions were met. You were worthy only if you acted in a certain way, behaved with dignity and propriety. When you were perfect.

Like Caspian. He was worthy, but you never were.

His father's chilly distance had always made that very clear. The opportunity to earn that love was gone now, along with his father, but that didn't mean he should stop trying. That was what he'd dedicated his life to. Trying to be worthy of the title he'd inherited.

He'd fashioned himself into a king his country would be proud of, and that had taken nearly everything he had. How could he also fashion himself into a good husband? A man worthy of

Inara's love? Being a king was a heavy enough burden. He didn't need to add to it.

He stared at her, a possessive, hungry anger boiling inside him, demanding to be let out. Demanding that he close the distance between them and take her in his arms, kiss that beautiful mouth, tell her that there would be no divorce—not now, not ever.

But he forced it aside. If he couldn't be what she wanted him to be, then he could hardly demand the same of her. Insisting that there would be no divorce would be the height of hypocrisy and he couldn't do that.

She's yours...

No, she wasn't. She'd proved herself a worthy queen, far more worthy than he deserved. It would be better to let her go.

Something in him felt as though it was being torn in two, but he ignored it, shoved the lid on his anger and his pain and let it boil dry until there was nothing left but the hard shell of a king.

He drew himself up. 'Very well,' he said. 'I won't insist. If a divorce is what you want, then that's what you'll have.'

Shock crossed her face, followed by a brief

flare of agony that drew an echo of pain from him too.

'Just like that, Cassius?' Her voice was hoarse and it was clear she hadn't expected him to agree. 'You give in just like that?'

He ignored the part of him that wanted to take her in his arms, soothe her hurts and tell her that he wanted to keep her for ever. But he couldn't do it. He couldn't bear the weight. The expectations of a king were crushing him already; the expectations of a husband would kill him.

'There's no point fighting about it.' He could hear his own voice, cool and calm, as if it were someone else's. 'I'll admit it's not what I want, but I won't stand in your way if you want to leave.'

She blinked again furiously and he could see tears behind the lenses of her glasses. They felt like knives to his soul. Yet another sign that he was doing the right thing, of course.

'What about us having no choice? If I'm pregnant then—'

'If you're pregnant then we'll cross that bridge when we come to it.' Something in him settled, hardened, became rigid. And he let it. 'In the meantime, I'll get the papers drawn up. If you require anything, anything at all, it's yours.'

Her mouth was soft and vulnerable, and tears trailed down her cheeks. 'Anything but your heart, right?'

'You don't want my heart, Inara,' he said. 'There's not much of it left. You deserve more than what I have to give you.'

She looked unbearably regal standing there in her blue gown with her hair loose, the crown glittering on her head, her chin lifted. Vulnerable, yes, but there was also a strength to her.

His people had accepted her, but she'd never be his queen. He'd find someone else, someone who wouldn't demand things from him. Expect things from him. Someone who'd accept what he had to give and never ask for more.

'You're right,' she said. 'I do deserve more. I deserve to be loved, and by you.'

Something in his heart tore, but he ignored that along with everything else. 'Find someone else, Inara. Someone better. Someone who doesn't have a crown to bear as well. I can only carry one thing, and I'm sorry, but that's my country. I can't carry you as well.'

She took a heaving breath, opened her mouth

to say something and then, clearly thinking better of it, pressed her lips together and looked away. She nodded, her pretty crown glittering in the light. 'Very well,' she said at last. 'If that's how it's going to be, then I'll require a flight to the Queen's Estate, please. Tonight.'

She didn't wait for him to respond. She simply walked to the door.

'I thought you were better than that,' he heard himself say, even though he hadn't meant to... even though he thought he felt nothing. 'I thought you at least would accept me for who I am.'

She paused, her hand on the door. 'This is not who you are, Cassius.'

'You're wrong. This *is* who I am. And if you can't accept that, then you're better off leaving.'

A tear trickled down her cheek. 'Perhaps you're right,' she said softly. 'Perhaps I am.'

Then she quietly opened the door and went out.

CHAPTER TWELVE

INARA PACKED A bag that night. She didn't take much—she'd come with nothing, so that was how she would leave. With nothing. There was nothing she wanted to take with her anyway. If she couldn't have him, she didn't want anything else.

Grief tore at her heart. Not so much grief for herself, though that was there too, but grief for him. For how he'd become so stiff and rigid before her eyes, the Prince she'd loved vanishing, becoming the King.

She hated the King.

Is that fair?

She grabbed some dresses at random and flung them into her suitcase. Her glasses were fogging up so she had to pause and take them off, rubbing at the lenses, tears still pouring down her cheeks.

Her heart wasn't just broken glass in her chest

in any more; it felt like barbed wire, cutting at her soul.

Whether it was fair or not, he was right about one thing. She deserved more than he could give her. She did. No one had loved her for her entire life and, now she knew what it felt like to have someone, she didn't want to do without it. And if it couldn't be him, then it would be someone else.

You don't want anyone else.

She ignored that voice as she tossed a T-shirt into her case. Somewhere out there would be someone who'd want her. Someone who wouldn't shut her out, who wouldn't blow hot and cold, who'd tell her unequivocally where she stood. Someone who'd love her the way she so desperately wanted to be loved.

It just wouldn't be him.

You're being as unfair to him as he is to you, demanding things of him that he doesn't know how to give. No wonder he thinks love is a burden. You're demanding he be the person he was back then, but he'll never be that man again.

'I thought you were better than that,' he'd said to her. 'I thought you'd accept me for who I am.'

Inara's throat felt tight and sore, the barbed wire in her heart twisting.

Maybe there was some truth in that. But what else could she do? Stand by and accept whatever he had to give her? Try and love the hard, distant man who wouldn't let himself be loved? Who viewed it as a burden?

Who viewed himself as a burden.

Tears slipped down her cheeks as it slowly became clear to her what she must do. She didn't want anyone else. She'd *never* want anyone else.

And she couldn't leave him. She couldn't reject the man he was now simply because he wouldn't give her what she wanted. Would she be any different from his father? From his parents, who'd made him feel that he was unworthy somehow?

And how would he ever learn that love wasn't a burden, wasn't a weight, wasn't an expectation he had to meet, unless she showed him?

Love wasn't conditional, but sometimes it required sacrifices. Sometimes it required compromises. So if she wanted him, she'd have to be the one to take that first step, because it was clear he couldn't. Not yet. In fact, he might never be able to take that step. But love wasn't just sacrifice, it was faith as well, and if you didn't have faith in love what else could you have faith in?

She had to be the one to set the example this time. And one day, he'd learn. Perhaps not right now, but some day.

She just had to hope that he would.

Cassius organised a helicopter to take Inara to the Queen's Estate, then stayed in his office to organize having the divorce papers drawn up. He didn't want her to wait a second longer, as staying married to him was obviously such a trial.

He told himself he felt nothing, that the shell he'd developed after his family had been killed had hardened. That it was part of him now. And he ignored the anger and pain and betrayal at how she'd walked out. Ignored, too, the deeper emotion that went with it. It was a hot, powerful current that couldn't be allowed to roam free.

Instead, he liaised with his legal team then drew himself up a schedule of what he had to do in the morning. Number one of which would be finding himself a new queen.

But what if Inara is pregnant? What will you do? How can you let her go?

He shoved back his chair, trying to ignore the questions tumbling round in his head. Trying to ignore the strength of the emotion inside him, desperate for release.

He *had* to let her go. He couldn't give her what she wanted. She deserved better.

There comes a point where you have to decide whether to let that be a stick you keep beating yourself with. Or you choose to let it go and accept who you are. Like I did. Like you taught me.

Her voice drifted through his head and he tried to shove it away.

She was wrong. He couldn't let those standards slip and he *had* accepted who he was. It was she who hadn't accepted it.

And if she did...if she just loved you...if she accepted you for who you were without you having to do a thing...why didn't anyone else?

But he couldn't go there, couldn't think about that.

Sleep was too far off, his mind far too active, so he left his office, heading through the quiet halls to his private study.

He opened the door and walked straight in.

Only to find Inara standing in front of the fireplace, still in her blue gown, her hands clasped tightly in front of her, her cheeks still wet.

Not gone to the Queen's Estate after all.

Shock rooted him to the spot, swiftly followed by a wild joy he couldn't quite shake.

'What are you doing here?' His voice was rough.

The expression on her face was raw with pain, open with longing. 'I can't leave you, love. I tried and I can't. Because you're right. I wanted the Prince, not the King. But that isn't love and I...wanted to show you that love isn't about expectations, and it isn't a weight. It's not a burden. Love is acceptance and...'

She swallowed. 'I love you, Cassius. I love you as the King as well as the Prince. I love the man you were and I love the man you are now. And so I'll stay here with you, for as long as you want me. You don't have to do anything. You don't have to be anyone. Just be you. You as you are, right now, is all I want.'

There was a roaring in his ears, as if someone had let off a bomb somewhere nearby and the sound of the explosion was still echoing.

You as you are, right now, is all I want.

That couldn't be true. It couldn't.

'You don't want that,' he said hoarsely. 'You can't want that. I'm…flawed, Inara. Don't you see? Don't you understand? If I don't have to do anything…if I don't have to be anyone…' He stopped, pain twisting in his heart at a truth he didn't want to face. 'Then why couldn't my father…?'

She crossed the room to him, coming to stand in front of him, her small hands lifting to take his face between them. The heat of her palms seared him all the way through.

'Didn't you ever think, love, that the problem wasn't you?' Her voice was soft and there was no hiding from the bright flame in her eyes. 'That the problem was him?'

How she understood what he was talking about, he didn't know, but she did. And he found he'd lifted his own hands, his fingers circling her wrists, pressing against the fragile bones, feeling her heat and her strength. 'How could it be him? He loved Caspian. He never had any issue—'

'It was never you, Cassius,' Inara said thickly. 'And if he couldn't see the kind, generous, wonderful man you actually are, the selfless, compassionate King you've become, then he was blind. And he was stupid. And he was wrong.'

He wanted to tell her that that couldn't be the truth, that it couldn't be as simple as that, but her grey eyes had gone luminous and everything he'd been going to say had gone clean out of his head.

'It's time to stop punishing yourself, my love,' she said quietly. 'Let your family go. You don't need to keep them here any longer. You have me now, and I'll keep you safe.'

Something inside him suddenly cracked apart, the hard shell he'd drawn around him shattering, letting out all the flawed emotions he'd been so desperate to keep inside. The grief and the guilt and the pain and the anger.

And, most of all, the love.

Because she'd stayed. She'd stayed. She'd stayed for *him*. She didn't want him to be anything else. She didn't demand it.

Love was sacrifice and duty, but love was also Inara—here, after he thought she'd left him. Inara, who'd accepted herself and who'd accepted him too. Who'd taught him that he could be himself, that he could be both king and prince. But, above all, a man.

A man who loved her.

Cassius let go of her wrists, sliding his hands down her arms, down her sides to her hips. Then he pulled her hard against him, every cell in his body craving her presence. Craving everything she had to give and more.

'Inara,' he whispered. 'Inara…' He had no other words.

But then she solved the problem by going up on her toes and kissing him. Making it clear that he didn't need to say a thing.

So he didn't try. Instead, he tore her gown away and took her down onto the floor of his study, telling her with his hands on her body and the kisses following in their wake, and with his sex as he eventually pushed inside her, what she meant to him.

He couldn't say the whole of what he felt; he didn't know how. But he could learn. He was willing.

So she taught him all she knew, a lesson that began that night in his study and continued on through all the years of their marriage—lessons in joy, in happiness. In comfort, and pleasure, and most important of all in love.

And eventually Cassius found the words to tell

her what he felt for her, how she'd freed him, how she'd changed him. How she made him more himself every day.

But by then he didn't need to.

She already knew.

EPILOGUE

INARA WANDERED OVER to the windows of her and Cassius's private study and peered out into the garden. Roman, their son, had disappeared yet again and his tutor was getting tetchy. Inara had an important meeting with one of her ministers that afternoon, but she wanted to find Roman first, plus she had something to tell Cassius.

Sure enough, the pair of them were outside, staring critically at one of the rose bushes. Cassius pointed at something and Roman, who was getting tall even at only eleven, frowned and nodded.

Inara smiled. Her son loved these moments with Cassius, both of them focused on soil conditions and pest control, and whether the flowers needed more fertiliser. It didn't happen often, as Cassius was very busy, but he always made time for his son, especially as the boy hated sitting still as much as his parents did.

In the corridor outside came the sound of girlish voices arguing. The twins were shouting about whose turn it was to be the prince in the game they were playing. Neither of them wanted to be the princess, to Inara's eternal amusement.

She turned from the window, thinking she might have to adjudicate before the hair pulling began, but then she heard the door to the garden open behind her. Roman dashed past to join his sisters in the corridor, and then a strong arm wrapped around her waist, a warm mouth pressing a kiss to the nape of her neck.

'Have I told you today that I love you?' Cassius murmured. 'I feel I haven't.'

Inara sighed, the warm contentment and joy she always felt in her husband's presence filling her as she leaned back against him. 'You have. Only an hour ago, in fact. But feel free to tell me again.'

'I love you, little one.' His mouth moved to the side of her neck, his hands beginning to roam. 'I love you for ever.'

'I'm glad.' A little bolt of excited happiness sparked inside her. 'Because I have something to tell you.'

'If it's about the twins and the frog they put in the nanny's—'

'No, it's not about the twins and the frog.' Inara turned in his arms and stared up into his beloved face.

His eyes were glowing the way they did when he wanted her, all smoky amber and heat, and his mouth was curving in that warm, wicked way. 'Then what is it? Be quick. I feel I might be about to ravish you in the garden if you're not careful.'

'I'm never careful; you should know that about me by now.' Inara smoothed the lapels of his jacket. 'How would you feel about being a father again?'

His smile was slow and devastating and full of joy, and even all these years later it still had the power to set her on fire. He bent his head and kissed her hard, then murmured against her mouth.

'I feel that nothing else would give me greater pleasure.'

It had been a long road, a difficult road, but they'd journeyed it together.

One by one he'd let go of his guilt and his grief, allowing his family finally to be free. Allowing himself to be free too. And, while that had been hard, it had also been worth it.

He was worth it. He always had been.

'Little one,' he said quietly. 'You make me so very happy. Every single day.'

* * * * *

LET'S TALK
Romance

For exclusive extracts, competitions
and special offers, find us online:

f facebook.com/millsandboon

◎ @millsandboonuk

🐦 @millsandboon

Or get in touch on 0844 844 1351*

For all the latest titles coming soon,
visit millsandboon.co.uk/nextmonth